D0949877

brave

Svetlana Chmakova

brave

SVETLANA CHMAKOVA

Coloring assistant: Melissa McCommon

Lettering: JuYoun Lee

JY
1290 Avenue of the Americas
New York, NY 10104

Visit us at yenpress.com
facebook.com/yenpress
twitter.com/yenpress
yenpress.tumblr.com
instagram.com/yenpress

First JY Edition: May 2017

JY is an imprint of Yen Press, LLC.
The JY name and logo are trademarks of Yen Press, LLC.

Library of Congress Control Number: 2017934376

Hardcover ISBN: 978-0-316-36317-4
Paperback ISBN: 978-0-316-36318-1

10 9 8 7 6 5

LSC-C

Printed in the United States of America

Table of Contents

CHAPTER 1

PEOPLE ARE OBLIVIOUS...

...BUT SO MANY DANGERS LURK!!

SUNSPOTS ARE THE BIG ONE...I'M STILL FIGURING THAT ONE OUT...BUT SAY...

...IF THERE'S AN EARTHQUAKE?

I KNOW **EXACTLY** WHAT TO DO.

AND FOR A TORNADO TOO!

...AND...OH! IF IT'S A ZOMBIE APOCALYPSE?

I HAVE A LIST OF **WARNING SIGNS** IN MY POCKET.

(IN THE SAME POCKET, I ALSO HAVE A PROTEIN BAR AND A GAME BOY. IN CASE I HAVE TO BARRICADE MYSELF IN THE MAINTENANCE ROOM...)

...THERE ARE MANY ZOMBIE WARNING SIGNS IN MY MATH CLASS...

URGH

I BETTER BE CAREFUL.

...OF COURSE, IT COULD JUST BE THAT THIS IS **MATH**...

...WITH MR. KRISTOFFER, THE MOST BORING AND EVIL MATH TEACHER IN THE **UNIVERSE**.

PAY ATTENTION, CLASS, OR IT'S EXTRA HOMEWORK AGAIN FOR EVERYONE!

I HAAAAATE MATH.

BUT MOM SAID I'LL NEED IT FOR WHAT I WANT TO BE —

AN **ASTRONAUT** AT **NASA!**

$$42 \div 5\tfrac{5}{8} = ?$$

UH...

UM...

IS...IT...

...67?

68!

...81?

NO, IT MOST CERTAINLY IS NOT!

NOOOO

NO.

!

NO...

THAT'S IT!! EXTRA HOMEWORK FOR EVERYONE!! TWENTY PROBLEMS BY TOMORROW!!

GRRRR

THANKS A LOT!

...

WTH, JENSEN?

AGAIN?

I WISH THE ZOMBIE SURVIVAL GUIDE COVERED SITUATIONS LIKE THIS...

RRRRING

GRUMBLE stupid jensen. GLARE

· · ·

· · ·

IT'S OKAY. NEXT CLASS WILL BE BETTER.

IT'S ENGLISH! I REALLY LIKE THE TEACHER, MISS LEE...

...AND I HAVE A FRIEND THERE, PENELOPE TORRES.

WE'RE IN THE ART CLUB TOGETHER.

I JUST NEED TO GET THERE WITHOUT—

!

HEY, FATSO.

WHEN ARE YOU GONNA LEARN FRACTIONS, PEA BRAIN?

IF WE HAVE TO DO **ANY MORE** HOMEWORK BECAUSE OF YOU, I'M GONNA MAKE YOU REGRET IT. GOT THAT?

I DIDN'T GET ANY GOOD PICTURES.

IT'S OKAY. WE'LL GET THOSE TROLLS NEXT TIME.

H-HI, GUYS!

HMPF

...THIS IS JENNY, AKILAH, AND FELIPE.

THEY RUN THE SCHOOL NEWSPAPER AND A POPULAR VLOG. **NO ONE** WANTS TO MESS WITH THEM.

C'MON, WE GOTTA GO.

SEE YOU LATER, JENSEN.

BYE...

...I WANT TO IMPRESS THEM **SO BADLY**...

GET THEM TO PUBLISH MY ARTICLE ABOUT SUNSPOTS...

JUST DROPPING OFF THIS ARTICLE ON MY WAY TO DISCOVER THE SECRETS OF ANCIENT MAYAN TEMPLES.

JENSEN, THIS IS FRONT-PAGE MATERIAL!! SUNSPOTS ARE REALLY THIS DANGEROUS?!! I MUST PRINT THIS IMMEDIATELY!!

"HEY, NO PROB, JENNY.

"ANYTIME YOU GUYS NEED AWESOME ARTICLES, JUST LET ME —"

OOF

HA HA HA

....!

UH! SORRY!

13

...PENELOPE TORRES?

HERE!

THAT'S HER! MY FRIEND FROM ART CLUB.

I THINK...SHE'S *DRAWING SOMETHING.*

STRETCH

JENSEN GRAHAM?

....!

UH, HERE!

JORGE RUIZ?

HERE.

...I'M GONNA SKETCH TOO.

I'VE BEEN ON A BIG SPACESHIP KICK LATELY...

NASA SAYS THEY NEED NEW SHIP DESIGNS, SO I—

MISS TORRES.

MR. GRAHAM.

PUT THOSE SKETCHES AWAY AND PAY ATTENTION PLEASE.

WE'RE STARTING ON GROUP PRESENTATIONS TODAY.

EVERYONE, PICK YOUR GROUPS NOW!

NO MORE THAN THREE PEOPLE PER GROUP AND NO FEWER THAN TWO, FOR OBVIOUS REASONS.

GROUP OF TWO?

THAT'S ME AND PENELOPE! I'M GONNA ASK...

HEY, PENELOPE! WANNA BE IN OUR GROUP?

YEAH, OKAY!

...

HEY, MATT! YOU, ME— GROUP?

OKAY.

MELISSA, YOU'RE IN MINE!

UH.

UM.

THERE'S... NO ONE ELSE I CAN ASK.

DO YOU HAVE A GROUP, JENSEN?

UH... N-NO...

OKAY, WHO'S GOT ROOM FOR JENSEN?

UH... NOT US!

WE'VE ALREADY GOT THREE.

US TOO.

I COULD... JUST BE MY OWN GROUP.

ALL RIGHT, I NEED A VOLUNTEER TO LEAVE THEIR GROUP TO BE JENSEN'S PARTNER!

I'LL DO IT, MISS LEE.

GREAT! THANK YOU, JORGE!

NOW, EACH GROUP WILL PICK A PRESENTATION TOPIC WHILE I HAND OUT THE GUIDELINES.

YAMMER CHATTE HA HA

BASEBALL.

H-HUH?

FOR THE TOPIC?

...O-OH!

Y-YEAH, OKAY.

...

...

...

HELP, MRS. PRATT, I HAVE TO PRETEND I KNOW BASEBALL!

TAKA TAKA

OH? HMM. LET'S SEE...

HOW ABOUT BASEBALL FOR IDIOTS?

—OOF, WHAT AN UNFORTUNATE TITLE.

I DON'T CARE!!

IT'S **PERFECT!**

CAN I HAVE IT, PLEASE?!!

YUS.

I **SO** GOT THIS.

...AND **THAT** IS HOW I WILL SAVE THE WORLD...

...BY BEING PREPARED FOR **ANYTHING.**

21

WE'RE MAKING MINI GAMES IN COMPUTER CLASS...

...PLAYING **VERY** BADLY IN MUSIC...

(BUT MR. HISAYA IS SO OLD, HE CAN BARELY HEAR THAT WE SOUND LIKE A TRAIN WRECK.)

...AND TRYING VERY, **VERY** HARD NOT TO FAIL SCIENCE.

—QUANTUM PHYSICS IS A FASCINATING FIELD WITH MANY APPLICATIONS...

...AND THEN...

...IT'S FINALLY...

TIC TOC TIC TOC

P R R I N G

SKIDD

WHO'S READY TO DRRRRAW?!

...TIME FOR ART CLUB!!

JENSEN, HA-HA! WE **STILL** HAVEN'T GOTTEN RID OF YOU?

HEY, CAPTAIN SUNSPOTS.

HEY, GUYS! WHAT ARE YOU ALL DRAWING?

CAN I SEEEE?

I FINISHED MY ELF MOTORCYCLE SQUAD, HEH-HEH!

OOOH

FELICITY, THEY'RE **NOT** ELVES IF THEY RIDE MOTORCYCLES!

WHAT?!

SO COOL

YES, THEY **ARE!**

ELVES RIDE HORSES! AND LIVE IN FORESTS!

SAYS *YOU*! *MINE* ARE BADASS BIKER ELVES.

OMG, YOU GUYS, STOP WHATEVER IT IS YOU ARE DOING!!!

...THEY DO LOOK LIKE ELVES...

PEPPI? WHA—

I HAVE THE BEST. NEWS.

JAIME AND I WERE JUST IN THE LIBRARY, AND—

WHAT, DID HE PROPOSE OR SOMETHING?

HA HA HA HA HA

...UGH, *NO*! STOPPIT, TESS!

YOU GUYS, WE WERE TALKING TO MRS. PRATT JUST NOW, AND SHE SAID...

...THAT THEY ARE GOING TO HAVE AN **ARTS FESTIVAL!**

RIGHT HERE AT OUR SCHOOL!!

WITH A COSTUME CONTEST, PRIZES, AND EVEN *AUTHOR* EVENTS!

AND GUESS WHO ONE OF THE AUTHORS IS—

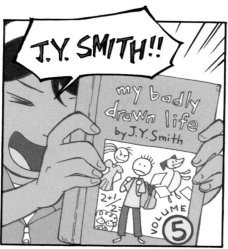

J.Y. SMITH!!

my badly drawn life by J.Y. Smith

VOLUME 5

SHUT UP!

I LOVE HIS BOOKS!

....!

WHAAA!?

I KNOW, RIGHT??

....?

AND ANOTHER GUEST IS INA CRUZ, THE MANGA ARTIST!!

SHE'S GONNA DO A DRAWING WORKSHOP!!

ARE YOU KIDDING ME RIGHT NOW?? I HAVE ALL OF INA'S BOOKS!

YES! YES! YESSS!

WHAT...WHAT IS THIS? ARE OUR BIRTHDAYS EARLY OR SOMETHING THIS YEAR?

MRS. PRATT SAID THEY NEED LOTS OF ART—THE LOGO, A POSTER, THANK-YOU CARDS FOR THE AUTHORS...

WHO WANTS TO HELP?

MEEEEEEEE!!

ME TOO!

DIBS ON THE THANK-YOU CARDS!

...I'LL HELP!

...I...

...ACTUALLY...

...HAVE NO IDEA WHO ANY OF THOSE AUTHORS ARE...

...BUT I CAN FIND OUT...?

LIBRARY

...BY INA CRUZ AND J.Y. SMITH? HMMM.

TAKA TAKA

THOSE ARE POPULAR BOOKS.

LOOKS LIKE ALL THE COPIES ARE OUT...

DO YOU WANT ME TO PUT YOU ON THE WAITING LIST?

UUHHH...

...YES.

...

SCHOOL'S SO EMPTY ALREADY.

...NO ZOMBIE APOCALYPSE AGAIN TODAY, HUH...? ...YAY?

BLEAH RRRG GRAR

I'D LURE ALL THE ZOMBIES TO THE CAFETERIA...

THAT'S TOO BAD. I HAVE AN **AWESOME** PLAN FOR THAT.

RAWR ARGH WAH

...AND THEN PROP UP THE DOOR WITH A FOLDING TABLE!!

BRREEP!

AUGH!

...JUST A TEXT FROM MOM...

THANKS FOR THE HEART ATTACK, MOM!

I THOUGHT THERE WAS A ZOMBIE IN MY POCKET...

29

...WELL, A ZOMBIE HAND... OR MAYBE...

...A ZOMBIE FOOT—

HUH?

IT'S *THEM!* WHY ARE THEY HERE SO LATE?

HEY...

IS THAT...?

HUH?

THEY SAW ME!!!

HEY, JENSEN!

COME OVER HERE!

CHAPTER 2

HUFF HUFF

HEY, JENSEN! WAIT UUUP!

PANT PANT

NOPE! NOPE, NOPE!

WHAT SHOULD I DO, WHAT SHOULD I DO?!

CAFETERIA

....!

...THE CAFETERIA!!

I...I CAN USE MY ZOMBIE PLAN!

...IT'S LOCKED?!

OH, JENSEEEN!

NO, NO, NO, NO!!

WHERE'D HE GO?

DOWN THE STAIRS?

....!

HUFF HUFF

THERE'S ONE...

... MORE... ...PLACE...

HUFF

GASP

NEWSPAPER OFFICE

...TO TRY...

J-JENNY? AKILAH?

I-IS ANYONE THERE?

BAM BAM

CLICK

...JENSEN?

AND SO —!

SHUFF SHUFF SHUFF

TAKA TAKA

HOW ABOUT THIS FOR THE...

TOO BLURRY.

I'M SAFE HERE.

FOSTER AND YANIC WOULD NEVER **DREAM** OF COMING DOWN HERE...

...BECAUSE THEN THEY'D HAVE TO DEAL WITH JENNY...

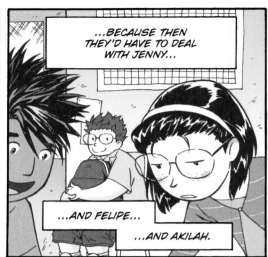

...AND FELIPE...

...AND AKILAH.

THESE THREE ARE LIKE A COMIC BOOK JUSTICE POWER TEAM.

JENNY IS THE CAPTAIN...

...AND AKILAH THE RIGHT-HAND COMMANDER...

...WHILE FELIPE IS LIKE THE ROGUE PILOT WHO CRASH-LANDS A LOT BUT ALWAYS COMPLETES HIS MISSION.

...ALSO, A SUPERVISING TEACHER, MRS. CRABBLER.

SSNRE

I DON'T KNOW WHAT SHE DOES.

SHE NAPS A LOT.

I WISH THE ART CLUB WAS STILL A PART OF THE NEWSPAPER CREW.

WE USED TO DO A MONTHLY COMIC NEWSLETTER FOR THE PAPER, BUT...

...WE GOOFED AROUND TOO MUCH AND DIDN'T GET OUR COMICS IN ON TIME...

DO YOU THINK JENNY WAS SERIOUS ABOUT CANCELING THE NEWSLETTER IF WE'RE LATE?

I-I GUESS WE'LL FIND OUT.

...SHE WAS SERIOUS.

THAT IS HOW WE FOUND OUT THAT ONE DOES *NOT MESS* WITH JENNY.

SO OMG CANCELED. P.S. i hate you.

...Y-YEAH.

I'M REALLY HOPING SHE FORGOT...SO I CAN SHOW HER MY SUNSPOTS ARTICLE...

HEY, JENSEN!

....!

WILL YOU HELP US PUT THESE FLYERS UP AROUND THE SCHOOL?

...

GLANCE GLANCE

...

...ARE YOU LOOKING FOR FOSTER AND YANIC?

....!

LOOKING? HA-HA, NO! NO.

JUST...JUST MAKING SURE THEY'RE NOT HERE.

THEY MUST BUG YOU A LOT, HUH?

....!

OH, UH...

...WELL, I MEAN, IT'S **FOSTER** AND **YANIC**. THEY BUG EVERYONE...

...SO...

...

...

POINT POINT

...JENSEN, WE COULD ACTUALLY USE YOUR HELP WITH A PROJECT OF OURS.

M-MY HELP?!

...THAT'S WHAT I SAID...

YES!!

WHATEVER YOU NEED!

GREAT. DROP BY AGAIN, UH—

TOMORROW? WHAT DO WE HAVE...?

TOMORROW'S **SUPER** BUSY. WE HAVE TO FINISH THE SURVEYS.

MAYBE NEXT WEEK THOUGH? FELIPE'S GOT A FREE DAY ON TUESDAY.

STAPLE STAPLE

THURSDAY!

UH, THURSDAY! I MEANT THURSDAY.

...FELIPE, NO, WHAT ARE YOU DOING?!

I SAID ONE FLYER EVERY TEN FEET...

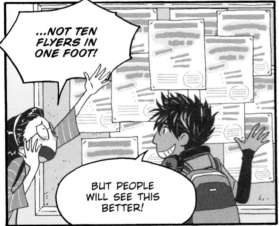

...NOT TEN FLYERS IN ONE FOOT!

BUT PEOPLE WILL SEE THIS BETTER!

NO, NO, NO, THIS IS TOO MUCH!

...WAIT, I LIKE THIS!

...YOU *DO*?

YEAH! IT STANDS OUT!

SEE? FELIPE DID GOOD!

NEWSPAPER SUBMISSIONS CALL!!! SUBMIT: •articles!! •photos!!

...SUBMISSION CALL?!

...I CAN SUBMIT MY SUNSPOTS ARTICLE!!

THE NEXT DAY.

START!

MATH IS EVIL AGAIN, ARGH!

EVERYONE, HAND IN THOSE TWENTY PROBLEMS FROM YESTERDAY *NOW*!

GROAN

UGH

...

NOOO, I WANT TO WORK ON MY ARTICLE...

BLAH BLAH BLAH BLAH BLAH BLAH BLAH BLAH

BUT I HAVE TO GET THROUGH IT...

...SO THAT, WHEN I'M A NASA ASTRONAUT ON THE INTERNATIONAL SPACE STATION, ON MY WAY TO JUPITER...

...I JUST WANT TO SAY TO EVERYONE DOWN THERE ON EARTH— MR. KRISTOFFER IS EVIL, AND HE WAS TOTALLY WRONG ABOUT ME!

what! is that jensen?!

CAPTAIN JENSEN GRAHM

HEH-HEH-HEH.

JENSEN.

JENSEN!

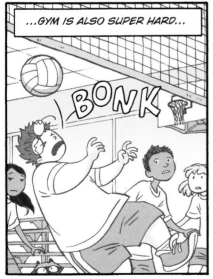

...GYM IS ALSO SUPER HARD...

BONK

...BUT AT LEAST MRS. RASHAD ISN'T EVIL.

FWEET

GOOD TRY, JENSEN!

EVERYONE, TAKE FIVE AND HAVE SOME WATER!

THANK YOU...

I HATE HAVING GYM BEFORE LUNCH.

I GET ALL TIRED AND SWEATY...

...AND THE GAME MONSTERS **NOTICE**.

DASH

...EWWW, WHO'S THE STINK BOMB?

HA HA HA

I HAVE TO STAY VIGILANT.

GLANCE GLANCE

I HAVEN'T SEEN YANIC AND FOSTER TODAY YET...WONDER IF THEY'RE OUT SICK?

THAT'D BE GREAT. I COULD GET TO LUNCH WITHOUT ENGAGING LURK MODE.

HACK COUGH

BUT WAIT.

WHAT IF THEY'RE **SICK AND IN SCHOOL?**

44

IT WOULD BE EASY, SINCE WE ALWAYS SIT TOGETHER AT LUNCH.

hi, jensen!

HEY, GUYS!

OH, LOOK, IT'S THE SUNSPOTS KID!

SAVED THE WORLD TODAY YET?

NOT YET! WORKING ON IT...

TESS AND I ALWAYS JOKE AROUND LIKE THIS. SHE'S REALLY FUNNY.

...OOOH, BOLOGNA SANDWICH TODAY!

SO...

RRUSTLE

...LOOKS LIKE EVERY DESIGN TASK FOR THE ART FEST IS SPOKEN FOR, YAY!

PING

THANKS FOR VOLUNTEERING, GUYS!

OH!

I WANNA HELP WITH THAT TOO!

WELL, THEN YOU SHOULD'VE RESPONDED TO THE GROUP CHAT, LIKE WE ASKED.

HUH?

WHAT CHAT?

THE GROUP CHAT FROM *YESTERDAY NIGHT*, JENSEN.

YESTERDAY?

I DIDN'T...

...SEE ANY CHAT...

...UH-OH. DID I MISS SOMETHING AGAIN?

...U-UH.

TESS?

I DON'T SEE HIM ON THE LIST YOU MADE.

I don't think he ever got invited...

...

...OH.

JENSEN, I AM *SO* SORRY!!

IT'S... IT'S OKAY.

I'M DOING THE POSTER WITH TESS AND NINA. DO YOU WANT TO HELP US?

OH! N-NO, THAT'S OKAY.

...

...ANYWAY!

DID YOU GUYS SEE THAT NEW TRAILER FOR *STAR WARS*?

OH! IS IT OUT?

...THIS IS SO AWKWARD.

...BUT, YAY, ENGLISH IS NEXT! I'M **SO** GLAD I HAVE A PARTNER FOR THAT PRESENTATION.

BASEBALL.

...EVEN IF IT'S THAT SPORTS DUDE, JORGE.

CLICK

HE **VOLUNTEERED** TO BE IN A GROUP WITH ME...

NO ONE DOES THAT!

...HE LOOKS LIKE HE COULD STOP AN ENTIRE ZOMBIE APOCALYPSE. **BY HIMSELF.**

...

RRRING

ENGLISH

THAT WAS THE BELL, JORGE. CAN YOU PUT THAT PHONE AWAY?

YES.

SORRY, MISS LEE.

....!

OKAY, EVERYONE, TODAY IS A WORK PERIOD FOR YOUR PRESENTATIONS!

OH NO!!

...THE BASEBALL BOOK!

I COMPLETELY FORGOT TO EVEN FLIP THROUGH IT!

I WANT YOU TO START HAMMERING OUT YOUR SUBTOPICS AND OUTLINE.

I'LL BE WALKING AROUND AND ANSWERING ANY QUESTIONS.

YAMMER CHATTE

HA HA

...

...WHY DIDN'T I EVEN **BRING THE BOOK?!**

ANY IDEAS FOR A SUBTOPIC?

....!

U-UH.

NOTHING. I GOT NOTHING!

...

UH...

I-I...

...

...ACTUALLY...

...DON'T KNOW MUCH...ABOUT BASEBALL?

...

OH.

OKAY.

WELL...

...BASEBALL'S PRETTY COOL.

HELP.

I THOUGHT THEY JUST HIT A BALL WITH A STICK!

BUT THERE ARE ALL THESE **RULES**!

WELL, ALL YOU REALLY NEED TO KNOW IS THAT GIANTS ARE THE BEST.

UH, *NO.* DODGERS ARE.

EXCUSE ME?? WHO'S GOT MORE WORLD SERIES TITLES?

TITLE, SHMITLE.

...ARGH, I DON'T UNDERSTAND ANY OF THIS.

FIFTEEN MINUTES LATER.

GUH

...STILL...CAN'T...

...UGH.

...I SHOULD DRAW!

IT'S ART CLUB, AFTER ALL.

WHAT IF WE USED THIS FONT?

IS THIS THE LOGO?

...

...OH YEAH, EVERYONE'S WORKING ON THE ARTS FESTIVAL STUFF.

WELL, I'M GOING TO WORK ON...

...

SAVING THE WORLD
(A.K.A. MY SUNSPOTS ARTICLE.)

FIFTEEN MINUTES LATER.

WRITING ARTICLES IS HAAAAARD...

I WISH I COULD JUST MAKE IT INTO A COMIC...

HEY, ARTCLUB

....!

HUFF HUFF

...

UUH.

HI, JENNY.

WHAT'S UP?

...I THOUGHT YOU HATED US NOW?

ugh.

I *DO.*

traitors.

YOU RUINED OUR LIVES FOR A **WEEK.**

BUT, UGH, WE HAVE AN EDITING EMERGENCY!!

S-SO I'M HERE, BEING NICE, TO SEE IF ONE OF YOU...

cough deadline-missing jerkfaces *cough*

...CAN HELP US OUT?

...

...

riiiiight...

WELL, WE'RE ALL DOING STUFF FOR THE ARTS FESTIVAL...

...EXCEPT FOR JENSEN.

...JENSEN!

PERFECT.

WE NEED YOU ANYWAY!

COME WITH ME QUICKLY

I-I NEED TO PACK UP MY STUFF...

PACK QUICKLY

O-OKAY!

THERE IS SOMETHING I SHOULD PROBABLY EXPLAIN ABOUT JENNY...

CHAPTER 3

I WAS REALLY CONFUSED AT FIRST, BECAUSE SHE SWITCHED BETWEEN THEM WITH NO WARNING.

GOT ONE!

OH, JENSEN, YAY!

HEEEY, SPACEMAN!

AKILAH, TELL HIM WHAT TO DO!!

I'M GONNA GET MIC'D UP.

AYE-AYE, CAPTAIN!

THANKS SO MUCH FOR HELPING US, JENSEN.

HOW'S TODAY BEEN FOR YOU?

....!

O-OH!

UH. GOOD! TODAY, I...

NO TIME FOR CHITCHAT, AKILAH!!

UGH, OKAY, OKAY!

COOL YOUR BOSSY PANTS.

...OKAY, BASICALLY, WE NEED AAALL OF THESE PHOTOS FORMATTED.

THERE'S THE FOLDER.

...AND I WROTE YOU THIS STEP-BY-STEP.

AKILAH, WE GOTTA DO THIS—ARE YOU READY?!

I'LL BE RIGHT THERE!

C'MON, DUDE, GET YOUR MIC ON!

DON'T "DUDE" ME!

....?

...?

I HOPE THAT HELPS. THANKS AGAIN!!!

FELIPE, IS THE PROMPTER READY?

....!

...WAIT.

ARE THEY...?

ALMOST!

...THEY **ARE!**

JENSEN, DON'T GET DISTRACTED. WE NEED THOSE PHOTOS!!!

Y-YES!

...THEY'RE FILMING AN EPISODE OF THEIR SHOW?? I DIDN'T KNOW THEY DID IT HERE!!

ANY COMMENT FOR BERRY SCOOP, GUYS?

DO IT AGAIN!

DO IT AGAIN!

I WOULD LIKE TO THANK MY FAMILY AND MY AWESOME ARMS.

I'M GOING TO GO AWAY TO TRAIN IN THE MOUNTAINS AND COME BACK FOR A REMATCH.

...DO YOU THINK HE'LL REEEALLY GO AWAY TO TRAIN IN THE MOUNTAINS?

I HOPE SO! THAT WOULD MEAN NO GEOGRAPHY UNTIL HE COMES BACK!

...AND NOW, IT'S TIME TO ANSWER SOME E-MAILS FROM OUR VIEWERS!

AMIRA WRITES, "DEAR BERRY SCOOP—"

...

...

...

...THIS IS SO AWESOME.

I WONDER...

CAN *I* GET ON THE SHOW?

COMING AT YOU LIVE WITH THE LATEST COVERAGE ON THE DANGER OF SUNSPOTS...

...IT'S JENSEN GRAHAM!

THANK YOU, JENNY. I'M UP HERE IN ZERO-GRAV, MONITOR!

CUT!

JENSEN, ARE YOU CROPPING THOSE PHOTOS?

HEY, WANT ME TO DO THAT LAST BIT?

. . . . !!

Y-YES! YES, I AM!

...OKAY, LET'S TRY THE E-MAILS AGAIN—ONE, TWO...

CLICK CLICK CLICK

TIC TOC
TIC TOC
TIC TOC

OKAY, I GOT ALL WE NEED AND CAN START EDITING!

GOOD! WE'VE GOT FORTY MINUTES LEFT!

I'LL DO THE SHOWNOTES.

I'LL FINISH THE SLIDE SHOW ARTICLE!

TIC TOC
TIC
TOC

I NEED SOMEONE TO PROOFREAD THIS!

OK.

JENNY, DO YOU WANT TO CUT THIS BIT?

UH.

JENNY, I THINK I JUST DELETED THE WHOLE FOLDER...?

WHAT?!

...OH, WAIT. NO, HERE IT IS.

TIC TOC TIC TOC

...UPLOADING...

...UPLOADING...

AND...

DONE!!

WITH TWO MINUTES TO SPARE, YOU GUYS!

YESSS! ANOTHER EPISODE OUT ON TIME!

YAAAAAY

...OOF.

...HMM, I GUESS THERE'S NO TIME TO DO JENSEN'S INTERVIEW TODAY...

JUST GIVE HIM THE HANDOUT. HE SHOULD READ THAT FIRST ANYWAY.

OH YEAH, GOOD IDEA!

....?

...INTERVIEW? HANDOUT...?

...WH-WHAT INTERVIEW?

FOR OUR PROJECT. YOU AGREED TO HELP YESTERDAY?

HERE'S SOME INFO ABOUT IT.

READ THIS AND COME BACK NEXT WEEK, 'KAY?

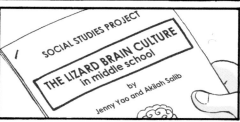

SOCIAL STUDIES PROJECT

THE LIZARD BRAIN CULTURE in middle school

by Jenny Yao and Akilah Salib

...LIZARD BRAIN...? WHAAA...

C'MON, GUYS, WE HAVE TO CLEAR OUT!

O-OKAY!

PHEW, WHAT A RACE TODAY...

THANKS FOR HELPING US AGAIN, JENSEN.

...O-OH, ANYTIME!

...ANYTIME?

REEEALLY?

CAREFUL, MAN, SHE'LL GIVE YOU A JOB, HA-HA!

THAT'S HOW SHE GOT ME.

I-I'D BE OKAY WITH THAT!

I LIKE TO HELP.

I WAS HELPING MY MOM WITH A FUND-RAISER, AND THEY SAID I—

SHH, YOU HAD ME AT "I LIKE TO HELP."

GIVE ME YOUR CELL NUMBER. I'LL TEXT YOU IF WE NEED HELP AGAIN.

. . . . !

THE NEXT DAY.

RRING

BERRYBROOK MIDDLE SCHOOL

GLEEEEEE!

...I'M PART OF THE NEWSPAPER CREW!!

...WELL, NOT **EXACTLY** PART OF IT, BUT...

...THEY WANT MY HELP!

JENNY EVEN TOOK MY NUMBER!

BEAM

BEAM

...

...NO TEXT YET.

...

I FEEL LIKE BATMAN, WAITING FOR THE BAT-SIGNAL.

TODAY'S LEVEL—

START!!

MATH.

JENSEN, YOU WILL LEARN MATH IF IT'S THE LAST THING I DO!!

UGHH... nasa... astronaut...

COMPUTERS.

FIELD TRIP SLIPS! DON'T FORGET!

OH, YEAH!

GEOGRAPHY.

...NO, I AM *NOT* LEAVING TO TRAIN IN THE MOUNTAINS.

SO, *YES*, YOU *DO* HAVE TO DO YOUR HOMEWORK!

LUNCH!!

I USED TO HAAATE LUNCH, BECAUSE I'D ALWAYS END UP SITTING ALONE...

IT'S SO DIFFERENT NOW THAT I HAVE ART FRIENDS! WONDER WHAT EVERYONE'S DRAWING TODAY!

HEY,
GU...

...!

...HUH?

THAT'S...
OUR USUAL
TABLE...

...BUT...
THOSE'RE
NOT MY
FRIENDS.

DID THEY...

...SIT
SOMEWHERE
ELSE?

SEARCH
SEARCH

I DON'T...

...SEE
THEM...

...ANYWHERE.

...

...

...WHERE'D DID THEY GO? DID I MISS SOMETHING...?

...

FEELS SO WEIRD TO JUST SIT BY MYSELF.

RRSTLE

...I'M GONNA READ THAT HANDOUT FROM JENNY AND AKILAH...

FLIP FLIP

...WHAT IS THIS LIZARD BRAIN STUFF?

...THERE'RE SO MANY PAGES...

...

I'LL, UH...

I'LL READ THIS LATER.

...INSTEAD!! I'LL WORK ON MY SUNSPOTS ARTICLE!

DIG DIG

I NEED TO FINISH THAT, SO I CAN...

...SUBMIT—

HEEY, IS THAT JENSEN?

IT IIIS!

....!

WHERE'RE YOUR NERD FRIENDS? THEY LEFT YOU ALL ALONE?

U-UH...

OF COURSE HE DOES!

WANT *US* TO KEEP YOU COMPANY?

UM.

OOOH, IS THAT YOUR SKETCHBOOK, JENSEN?

HA HA!

YOINK

WHOA!

THAT'S THE WORST-DRAWN *STAR TREK* FANART I'VE EVER SEEN!

...TH-THAT'S NOT... IT'S NOT *STAR TREK*!

IT'S FOR MY SUNSPOTS ARTICLE!

SUNSPOTS?

WHAT'S THAT SUPPOSED—

—TO...

...BE—

CRAP, IT'S JORGE!

IT'S THE FOURTH TIME TODAY!! IS HE FOLLOWING US?

AGAIN?!

SHF

LET'S SIT OVER THERE.

CRAP, NOW THEY'RE ALL COMING OVER?!

WHAT IS THIS, NEIGHBORHOOD WATCH?!! WHAT SHOULD WE DOOOO?

JUST PLAY IT COOL, PLAY IT COOL...

HI THERE, NEW GUY!

I'M OLIVIA!

WHAT'S YOUR NAME?

...

U-UH.

JENSEN.

NICE TO MEET YOU, UH JENSEN!

HA HA

S-SO, UH...

...E-EVERYONE SAW THE GAME LAST NIGHT, RIGHT?

HAH! IF YOU CAN CALL THAT A GAME.

. . .

WHAT IS EVEN HAPPENING RIGHT NOW??

I'M EATING LUNCH WITH THE GAME MONSTERS?!

...

...

WHAT KIND OF BIZARRO ALTERNATE UNIVERSE LEVEL IS THIS?

WAAA...

DAZE

...I JUST HEARD MORE ABOUT SPORTS IN ONE HOUR THAN I HAVE IN **MY LIFE.**

...OLIVIA SAID THEY WERE ALL FROM THE ATHLETICS CLUB.

...I GUESS SPORTS ARE...

...KINDA LIKE THEIR STAR TREK?

HUH.

ART CLUB.

...!

...THERE YOU GUYS ARE!

75

WHERE'D YOU GO AT LUNCH?

I WAS LOOKING FOR YOU ALL!

OH, THE WEATHER WAS SO NICE, WE WENT AND HAD A PICNIC OUTSIDE.

...A PICNIC! ...I LOVE PICNICS...

DON'T FEEL BAD, JENSEN. THEY DITCHED ME TOO.

WE DITCHED *YOU*?

YOU'RE THE ONE WHO DITCHED *US* TO BE WITH YOUR SCIENCE *BOYFRIEND!*

WH-WHA...?

W-WE'RE JUST WORKING ON A PROJECT TOGETHER!

SURE.

A PROJECT OF... LOOOOVE!

ARGH! NO!

CAN WE FOCUS ON OUR STUFF FOR THE ARTS FESTIVAL, PLEASE?

WE CANNOT SCREW IT UP LIKE WE DID THE COMICS NEWSLETTER, OKAY?

....?

BZZ

....!

...A TEXT FROM JENNY!

SO, JENSEN...

...I KNOW HOW BUMMED YOU WERE ABOUT GETTING LEFT OUT OF THE FESTIVAL PREP...

...SO HOW WOULD YOU LIKE TO HELP ME PICK A FONT FOR THE—

U-UH, ACTUALLY, I GOTTA RUN! JENNY WANTS ME TO HELP OUT AGAIN.

BYE!!

....!

...WELL.

ISN'T JENSEN SUDDENLY SPECIAL.

CHAPTER 4

TAPA TAPA TAP

I AM THE NIGHT.

LIKE A SWIFT SHADOW...

...I COME TO THE RESCUE OF THOSE IN NEED!

JENSEN!!

HUFF HUFF

...HEY, GUYS! YOU CALLED?

♪

PERFECT, COME OVER HERE.

SEE THOSE STACKS? THEY NEED TO BE SORTED TOGETHER AND STAPLED IN THREES, OKAY?

LET ME KNOW IF YOU HAVE QUESTIONS!

...OH.

...

OKAY.

...THIS IS NOT A VERY EXCITING RESCUE.

STAPLE

H-HEY, WAIT.

THESE PAGES ARE MORE OF THAT LIZARD BRAIN STUFF!

W-WAS I SUPPOSED TO READ THAT FOR TODAY...??

B-BECAUSE I HAVEN'T...

...OKAY, THAT'S DONE! WHAT'S NEXT ON THE TO-DO LIST?

...JENSEN'S HERE—WANNA DO HIS INTERVIEW?

....!

NO! NO, NO...

HMM... NO.

PHEW.

WE STILL HAVE TO FINALIZE THE ARTICLE TOPICS FOR THIS ISSUE.

UGH, I HATE THIS PART.

ARE YOU GOING TO BE DIFFICULT AGAIN?

ONLY IF YOU ARE.

C'MON, JUST ADMIT ALL MY CHOICES ARE *RIGHT*!

MAKE ME.

RUSTLE

STAPLE

ALL YOUR CHOICES ARE TOO *SAFE*!

YOU TOTALLY CUT ALL THE *IMPORTANT* STUFF!

PFFFT, I DO NOT.

...LIKE WHAT?

LIKE MY DRAMA CLUB STORY IDEA!

WE NEED TO PRINT SOMETHING ABOUT THAT!

...DRAMA IN A MIDDLE SCHOOL DRAMA CLUB— ARE YOU SERIOUS?

THAT'S JUST GOSSIP. IT'S NOT—

STAPLE

RUSTLE

NO, NO, NO!

TEACHER FAVORITISM IN A MIDDLE SCHOOL DRAMA CLUB! *NEPOTISM*, JENNY!

STAPLE RUSTLE

...

...

...WH-WHAT'S "NEPOTISM"?

...WHAT? ARE WE LOOKING AT THE SAME STORY? LOOK HERE.

"JAZMINE, THE SCHOOL PLAY LEAD, MISSES ONE TOO MANY REHEARSALS; MRS. BLOOM REPLACES HER WITH MICHELLE; JAZMINE IS FURIOUS."

STUPID BUT *FAIR*. WHERE DO YOU SEE NEPOTISM?

OKAY, FIRST?

JAZMINE ONLY MISSED *ONE* REHEARSAL...

...BECAUSE HER *MOM* WAS IN THE HOSPITAL.

AND SECOND?

MICHELLE? SHE'S MRS. BLOOM'S RICH COUSIN'S *NIECE*.

THEY'RE... FAMILY?

YES!

AND MRS. BLOOM HAS A HISTORY OF GIVING RICH KIDS BETTER ROLES SO THAT THEIR PARENTS GIVE MONEY TO THE PRODUCTION!

HOW IS THAT *FAIR*?

JAZMINE WORKED HER HEART OUT FOR THAT ROLE!

AND SHE DOESN'T GET TO PLAY IT BECAUSE HER FAMILY'S NOT RICH!

WE **HAVE** TO RUN **SOMETHING** ABOUT THIS!

HMM...

THAT'D BE QUITE AN ACCUSATION.

WE HAVE TO...

...CONSULT THE ORACLE.

WAIT, WHAT? WAIT, WAAAIT, NO...

DO WE **HAVE** TO?

YES.

THIS IS BIG.

...

ORACLE.

...SHE'S SLEEPING AGAIN.

....!

C'MON, MRS. CRABBLER, WAKE UP!! WE HAVE A QUESTION!

snork

retirement?...

NO, YOU'RE NOT RETIRED YET! PLEASE WAKE UP!

wha...

HMPF

so noisy...

...WHAT?

WHAT IS THIS MESS?

...HUH?

THAT'S JUST OUR RESEARCH. IT'S NOT—

YOU HAVE TO ALWAYS ORGANIZE YOUR RESEARCH, LADIES!

LET ME SHOW YOU HOW BEST TO.

NO! NONONO WE JUST HAVE ONE QUESTION

...AN ORGANIZED DESK MAKES FOR AN ORGANIZED MIND!

NOOOOUYOOOOO

JUST ONE QUESTION

STOP!! ARGH

TWO HOURS LATER.

THERE.

SPARKLE SPARKLE

NOW THEN, WHAT WAS YOUR QUESTION?

...

IT'S LATE, AND WE HAVE TO GO HOME NOW.

...WHY DO YOU CALL HER "THE ORACLE"?

BECAUSE SHE TELLS US WHAT WE CAN AND CAN'T PUBLISH...

UGH, WE JUST LOST AN ENTIRE AFTERNOON!

JENSEN, DID YOU AT LEAST FINISH STAPLING THE SURVEYS?

YES, I DID!!

OH, **GOOD.**

AND I FINISHED THE ROUGH CUT OF THE OUTTAKES!

YOU DID?!

THANKS, YOU GUYS! YOU'RE LIFESAVERS!

TOMORROW, WE TRY, TRY AGAIN!

..."WE"?

DOES...DOES THAT MEAN ME TOO...?

MAYBE...?

RRRING

...IT DID.

IT DID MEAN ME!

BERRYBROOK MID

IT'S BEEN A COUPLE OF WEEKS NOW...

PING!

...BUT I STILL GET TEXTS FROM JENNY TO COME HELP.

IT'S MOSTLY SMALL STUFF...

YOU GUYS CALLED?

JENSEN! YEAH! THESE NEED FOLDING.

...BUT I DON'T CARE...

FOLD FOLD

...BECAUSE THEN I'M PART OF THE CREW!

(KINDA, SORTA...)

...IT'S NICE I CAN GO THERE...

...BECAUSE ART CLUB IS NOT AS FUN AS IT USED TO BE...

bicker bicker

HI, GU—

ugh!

WHY IS THE DATE WRONG?! YOU WERE SUPPOSED TO CHECK IT!

NO, YOU WERE!

JENSEN, YOU'RE IN THE WAY!

MOVE MOVE

sorry, sorry!!

...I TRY NOT TO BUG THEM TOO MUCH.

O-OKAY, I'LL JUST BE IN THE BACK.

...MATH IS STILL EVIL, UGH...

...EVERYONE, HAND IN YOUR PRACTICE TESTS NOW!

THAT MEANS **YOU** TOO, JENSEN!

ALMOST... DONE...

LAST... QUESTION...

...AND THERE IS STILL THE USUAL DAILY GAUNTLET.

HEY JENSEEEN!

...!

NO NO NO

BUT NOW, THE PRIZE AT THE END IS...

PING!

...THE NEWSPAPER!

THEY ARE SO BUSY, I THINK THEY FORGOT ABOUT THAT LIZARD BRAIN INTERVIEW...

COME ON, COME ON, CLOCK'S TICKING!

...WHICH IS GOOD, BECAUSE I **STILL** HAVEN'T READ THAT HANDOUT.

JENSEN! NO DAYDREAMING!

TICK-TOCK!

I'M ALSO GETTING TO KNOW THE NEWSPAPER CREW BETTER.

AKILAH LOOOOVES JOURNALISM. SHE'S CONSTANTLY REPORTING SOMETHING.

RRING RRING

HELLO, BERRYBROOK PD? I'M FROM A LOCAL PAPER CALLING FOR COMMENT ABOUT THE VANDAL CASE.

HER DREAM IS TO WORK FOR THE NEW YORK TIMES.

JENNY'S ~~DREAM~~ LIFE GOAL IS TO RUN IT.

SHRUG

...OR START MY OWN MEDIA EMPIRE. WE'LL SEE.

FELIPE'S CURRENT GOAL IS TO SEE HOW MANY STAIRS HE CAN JUMP AT ONCE ON HIS SKATEBOARD.

GONNA FLY LIKE AN EAGLE, YO.

UGH, STOP BEING STUPID, JENSEN.

...FRIEND-FIGHT!

IS THAT WHAT TESSA AND I DO?

ANOTHER SCHOOL DAY...

START

BERRYBROOK M

RRRING

JENSEN, STOP DRAWING SPACESHIPS AND PAY ATTENTION!

H-HOW DOES HE KNOW?!

I WILL NOW RETURN YOUR PRACTICE TESTS FROM YESTERDAY!

...HUH?

IS YOUR MOM STILL ABLE TO HELP YOU WITH HOMEWORK?

...OH.

UM. NO...

SH-SHE GOT MOVED TO A LATER SHIFT... AND OVERTIME... S-SO...

I SEE.

...

TAKKA TAK

TAKKA

ALL RIGHT, THEN I'M SIGNING YOU UP FOR MY TUTORING GROUP.

....!

WE MEET EVERY DAY AFTER SCHOOL IN THIS ROOM.

YOU'LL START TODAY.

T-TODAY?!

BUT I HAVE ART CLUB! A-AND NEWSPAPER!

JENSEN, YOU'RE IN DANGER OF FAILING THIS CLASS.

THEY'LL HAVE TO SPARE YOU FOR A WHILE.

ENGLISH CLASS
(WORK PERIOD AT THE LIBRARY.)

GLOOM

...

...

...

DUDE,
DID YOUR
DOG DIE OR
SOMETHING?

...

I-I...

I'm failing math...

...and...I have to...

...go to a...
...a tutoring group...

...instead of
art club...

AH.

...

BUMMER.

...TUTORING'S
GOOD THOUGH.

I GOT SOME FOR
SCIENCE. REALLY
SAVED MY BUTT.

R-REALLY?

YEAH.
THAT STUFF,
LIKE, MAKES
SENSE NOW.

HUH! MAYBE IT
WON'T BE SO BAD.

...

THOUGH,
I'LL STILL BE
MISSING ART
CLUB...

I'M WORRIED MY
ART FRIENDS MIGHT
FORGET ABOUT
ME...AGAIN...

...

...THEY **FORGET** ABOUT YOU?

...THOSE DON'T SOUND LIKE FRIENDS.

NO, NO, IT'S NOT LIKE THAT! THEY'RE JUST... BUSY. LOTS TO DO...

...

...IF THEY'RE FRIENDS, THEN THEY'VE GOT YOUR BACK...

...WHETHER YOU'RE THERE OR NOT.

...

FRIENDS WON'T "FORGET" ABOUT YOU.

...OH.

RRING

LIBRARY

JORGE IS **SO COOL**.

LATER.

BYE!

HE'S ALWAYS SUPER NICE...

...AND I NOTICED THAT—

...IS THERE A PROBLEM HERE?

—HE'S KINDA LIKE THE SCHOOL SHERIFF.

HIM AND OLIVIA BOTH, ALWAYS LOOKING OUT FOR PEOPLE...

ARE YOU OKAY?

SNFFL

...

KEEP WALKING, BUDDY.

...I WONDER IF THEY'D WANT TO BE ON MY ZOMBIE SURVIVAL TEAM...

RAWR

RAWR

RAWR

...THE NEWSPAPER CREW! WHO'RE THEY TALKING TO?

...

...AH!

HEY, JENSEN!

NEED YOU TO COME OVER AGAIN TODAY AFTER SCHOOL.

WE'RE FINALLY DOING YOUR INTERVIEW, SO DON'T BE LATE.

?

...INTERVIEW?!

....!

I STILL HAVEN'T READ THAT HANDOUT!!

U-UH!

A-ACTUALLY...

...I CAN'T!

TODAY...

...I HAVE MATH TUTORING?

OH.

UHHH, OKAY...

HOW ABOUT TOMORROW, DURING LUNCH...?

CAN YOU COME THEN?

YESSS, I'LL BE THERE!

...TOMORROW AT LUNCH? THIS SHOULD TOTALLY GIVE ME ENOUGH TIME TO READ IT...

...BUT BEFORE TOMORROW...

NEWSPAR ART CLU

MATH TUTORING

...I STILL HAVE TO MAKE IT THROUGH TODAY'S SURPRISE BONUS LEVEL.

RRRING

I SURE HOPE JORGE'S RIGHT...

...AND THIS WILL HELP SAVE MY BUTT.

H-HELLO?

AH, JENSEN!

GOOD, YOU MADE IT.

YOU'RE IN GROUP TWO TODAY, AND YOUR TUTOR IS AARON.

THAT'S ME!

HEY. ☺

WHATEVER QUESTIONS AARON CAN'T ANSWER, YOU CAN ASK ME.

GO AHEAD AND MEET YOUR GROUP.

SO, JENSEN, RIGHT? HAVE YOU EVER BEEN IN A TUTORING GROUP BEFORE?

UH, NO...

WELL, WE DON'T BITE.

....!

WELL, MAYBE YANIC DOES.

BUT HE IS OFF-DUTY AND LEARNING MATH, LIKE EVERYONE ELSE.

....!

JENSEN?!

UH.

CHAPTER 5

RUSTLE RUSTLE

OH, WHOOPS, I FORGOT THE WORK SHEETS.

BE RIGHT BACK!

....!

. . .

THIS IS SO WEIRD.

SHOULD I SAY SOMETHING?

UH...

H-HELLO.

HOW'S IT GOING?

....!

. . .

FINE.

WHATEVER.

TWRL

TWRL

...HOW ARE YOU DOING THAT?

...WHA—?

OH.

I DUNNO.

IT'S PRETTY EASY.

FLING

· · ·

u u
· · · ·

ALL RIGHT, HERE THEY ARE!

WHO'S READY TO LEARN SOME MATH?

WHY IS YANIC BEING SO WEIRD?

MAYBE THIS TUTORING THING WASN'T SUCH A GOOD IDEA...

...ON THE OTHER HAND, WOW, AARON'S REALLY GOOD AT EXPLAINING.

OHHH.

...EVEN YANIC'S LISTENING.

...THOUGH, VICKIE SEEMS REALLY DISTRACTED.

TWRL

WHY'S SHE HERE ANYWAY? I THOUGHT SHE HAD GOOD MARKS?

...

...WOW, MY HOMEWORK MAKES SENSE FOR THE FIRST TIME IN MONTHS.

BEAM

BLEAHHH

YANIC, JENSEN, THIS IS NOT A TONGUE-MEASURING CONTEST! ROLL THOSE BACK UP!

SEE YOU GUYS SAME TIME TOMORROW!

THANKS, AARON!

...

...

SEE YOU TOMOR—

DON'T TALK TO ME.

...

...I WISH THERE WAS TUTORING FOR MIDDLE SCHOOL LIFE...BECAUSE THAT STILL DOESN'T MAKE SENSE.

BERRYBROOK MIDD

BLAH BLAH BLAH BLAH BLAH

$\frac{3}{16} = 0.1875$

I'M PRETTY EXCITED ABOUT TUTORING NOW.

I GOTTA READ THAT LIZARD BRAIN THING!

....!

HA HA HA

...NOOO, I NEED TO GO THAT WAY!

WHY AREN'T THEY GOING TO CLASS?!

I'LL HAVE TO GO AROUND.

HA HA HA

....!

...NO!

GAME MONSTERS *BOTH WAYS?*

UH... UH...

...

...W-WELL, WE'VE BEEN... IN TUTORING GROUP TOGETHER...

...SO MAYBE...

...THIS WAY?

WELL, LOOK WHO IT IS!

DUMBO THE SCIENTIST!

ARGH, WRONG CHOICE!

IS IT TRUE THAT YOU NEED TUTORING?

I THOUGHT YOU NERDS ARE SUPPOSED TO BE SMART!

U-UM. I HAVE TO GO.

AW, COME ON, STAY AND CHAT!

GRAB

...OH! JORGE! THERE YOU ARE!

TURN

...HUH?

WHERE?

DASH

HA HA

YEAH, I TOTALLY MADE THAT UP. I DON'T KNOW WHERE HE IS.

BUT IT WORKED!!

NEW DEFENSE STRATEGY—UNLOCKED!

RING

LUNCH.

A SPOT...

A SPOT...

...OUTSIDE?

YES! PLENTY OF SPOTS!

...OKAY, TEN MINUTES TO READ LIZARD BRAIN CULTURE, PAGE ONE OF...

...UGH, OF TEN?? THERE ARE TEN PAGES?

...OKAY, OKAY. HERE GOES.

"THE HUMAN BRAIN IS A COMPLEX SYSTEM OF CELLS AND NEURAL CONNECTIONS WHICH ARE STILL NOT WELL-UNDERSTOOD.

... · · ·

...UH.

RIGHT.

"FOR EXAMPLE, WHILE THE R-COMPLEX IS RESPONSIBLE FOR BASIC SURVAaaaa

I CAN'T. I CAN'T READ THIS IN TEN MINUTES.

FLIP FLIP FLIP

WHY ARE THERE SO MANY PAGES...?

ARD BRAIN INSTINC

· TERRITORIALITY, HOARDING OF RESOURCES

· AGGRESSION, DOMINANCE

I AM BEST!! BOW TO ME!!

RRR! MINE! NO TOUCHIE!

· FEAR/SELF-DEF

OH HEY, WHAT'S THIS?

NSTINCTS

· AGGRESSION, DOMINANCE

I AM BEST!! BOW TO ME!!

HA-HA, THIS ANGRY ONE LOOKS LIKE YANIC!

! ....

DING BZZ

JENSEN, WHERE ARE YOU?!

DASH!

JENSEN!!

FINALLY!!

S-SORRY!

GET OVER THERE!

FELIPE, MIC HIM UP!

AKILAH, DO YOU HAVE THE QUESTIONS?

YES, YES, CAPTAIN McBOSSY.

WE ONLY HAVE TWENTY MINUTES LEFT!!

HOLD STILL.

SH-SHOULD I TELL THEM THAT I DIDN'T READ THE —

...TOO LATE.

ROLL IT!

THIS IS CASE STUDY NUMBER TWELVE...

...FOR "BULLYING CULTURE: THE LIZARD BRAIN SABOTAGE OF CIVILIZED SOCIETY."

°REC

12

"LIZARD BRAIN SABOTAGE"?

...

STUDY PARTICIPANT IS TWELVE-YEAR-OLD JENSEN GRAHAM, VICTIM OF BULLYING.

HUH?

DOES SHE MEAN ME?

JENSEN, CAN YOU SHARE SOME EXAMPLES HOW LIZARD BRAIN BEHAVIORS AFFECT YOUR DAILY LIFE?

...

U-UH.

...I CAN'T. I HAVE TO CONFESS.

U-UM.

WH-WHAT'S LIZARD BRAIN?

I, UH, I DIDN'T ACTUALLY READ THE... THE THING?

...

YOU...

YOU...DIDN'T?

YOU DIDN'T READ...

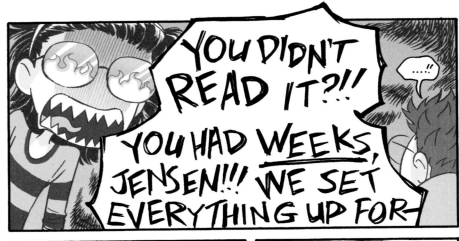

YOU DIDN'T READ IT?!!

YOU HAD WEEKS, JENSEN!!! WE SET EVERYTHING UP FOR—

....."

THIS INTERVIEW AND YOU—

...SO, JENSEN, WHAT JENNY IS CURRENTLY EXHIBITING IS A LIZARD BRAIN REACTION.

SIGH...

BETTER STOP THE RECORDING, FELIPE.

ALSO SOME SPECIAL EFFECTS.

INSTEAD OF RATIONAL PROBLEM-SOLVING, JENNY HAS REACTED WITH RAGE...

...A PRIMAL DEFENSE MECHANISM AGAINST DISTURBANCE OF CONTROL OF ONE'S ENVIRONMENT.

GLARE

STOPPIT, JENNY, 'KAY?

WHAT

THIS IS NOT RAGE THIS IS RIGHTEOUS INDIGNAT

J-JENNY HAS A LIZARD BRAIN??!

NO! UH...

WELL, UM...

OH BOY...

UM, OKAY, SO...UH...

THE THEORY WE ARE EXPLORING HERE IS THAT EVERY HUMAN IS BORN WITH, LIKE, A PRERECORDED SET OF SURVIVAL INSTINCTS, RIGHT?

REALLY BASIC STUFF LIKE—

"HUNGRY! FIND FOOD!" OR "DANGER! ACTIVATE DEFENSE MODE. UGH!"

grumble

GLARE

...LIKE YOU'RE DOING RIGHT NOW. "DANGER! ANGRY JENNY! STAY AWAY!"

ACCORDING TO OUR RESEARCH, *EVERYONE* HAS THESE BASIC SURVIVAL REACTIONS SINCE *FOREVER*.

WE'RE CALLING THAT THE "LIZARD" OR "TROGLODYTIC" BRAIN.

RAWR

113

AND EVEN THOUGH HUMANS ALSO HAVE *HIGHER* BRAIN FUNCTIONS—

—STUFF THAT LETS US CREATE ART, BUILD AMAZING THINGS, FLY SPACESHIPS—

—THE TROGLODYTIC BRAIN IS STILL THERE TOO!!! SENDING ALL SORTS OF "HEY! DO THIS TO SURVIVE!" SIGNALS.

BULLYING IS A TROGLODYTIC TACTIC! TRYING TO GET POWER BY PUSHING EVERYONE DOWN, TO SHOW HOW "TOP DOG" YOU ARE.

...THAT'S WHAT JENNY WAS BASICALLY ASKING YOU. "HOW DOES BEING BULLIED AFFECT YOUR LIFE?"

OHHHH!

S-SO...

...LET'S TRY THIS AGAIN.

HOW DOES BEING BULLIED AFFECT YOUR LIFE, JENSEN?

O-OH, ACTUALLY, I'M NOT?

BEING BULLIED?

WHAT?

YES. YES, YOU ARE.

THEY'RE CONSTANTLY HARASSING YOU.

TWITCH

OH, NO, NO!

THEY'VE NEVER CAUGHT ME! I'M TOO FAST!

...DUDE, THEY CALL YOU **NAMES**. THAT'S VERBAL BULLYING.

....!

UH...

WELL...

"STICKS AND STONES CAN BREAK MY BONES, BUT WORDS WILL NEVER HURT ME!"

AAAAA

...!

...JENSEN, WORDS CAN **TOTALLY** HURT YOU.

WORDS CAN

SAVE YOUR BREATH, LADY.

I'M GONNA GIVE HIM THE BULLYING CULTURE SURVEY.

JENSEN, IT HAS AN INFO SHEET TOO, ON THE THREE TYPES OF BULLYING.

I'M NOT...

THEY'RE **WRONG.**

...OH.

HERE'S THE SURVEY.

CHECK ALL THAT APPLY

Do you experience **repeated** instances of:

1. Denigrating nicknames
   ○ **yes** ○ **no** ○ **maybe**

2. Mean jokes at your expense
   ○ **yes** ○ **no** ○ **maybe**

3. Intimidation/threats
   ○ **yes** ○ **no** ○ **maybe**

physical hurt to you or your things
   ○ **yes** ○ **no** ○ **maybe**

TH-THESE DON'T APPLY TO ME...

HA HA CHATTER HE

...

...DO THEY?

COMPUTER CLASS.

TAKA TAKA TAK

...

BAND CLASS.

AFTER SCHOOL, HALLWAY.

HAHA edge edge

...I WAS RIGHT!

AS LONG AS I'M CAREFUL, EVERYTHING'S FINE!

PEOPLE JUST **IGNORE** ME, SO THAT'S A "NO" FOR ALL THESE QUES—

OH! THERE'S ONE MORE PAGE.

12. Do you have someone who will save a seat for you? Or do you feel isolated/left out?
○ **yes**   ○ **no**   ○ **maybe**

. . .

MATH TUTORING GROUP.

Be back in 15 min— Mr. K.

WHAT A WEIRD LEVEL TODAY...

SO TIRED NOW. WANNA GO HOME.

SLAM

HEY, DUMBO.

SIT

FUNNY JOKE ABOUT JORGE TODAY.

DID YOU COME UP WITH THAT YOURSELF, OR DID HE WRITE IT FOR YOU?

...AAAND YANIC IS BACK TO HIS OLD SELF.

HEY.

HEY.

ARE YOU GONNA SAY SOMETHING?

NOPE!

OKAY, LOOKS LIKE VICKIE DIDN'T MAKE IT TODAY...

LET'S GO AHEAD AND START.

HEEEY, IT'S THE AMAZING BIONIC MAN!

HALF MAN, HALF CRUTCH!

....!

HA.

HA.

REAL CLASSY, YANIC.

THESE ARE TODAY'S WORK SHEETS. WE'LL START WITH THESE SAMPLES—

FLIP FLIP

...YEAH, YEAH, YEAH.

OKAY.

BUT HOW ABOUT...

...WE DO *MY* HOMEWORK FIRST? I GOT A BASEBALL GAME TO GET TO.

....!

...UH, NO.

JENSEN IS MISSING HIS ACTIVITIES TOO. IT WOULDN'T BE FAIR.

NOW, LET'S TURN TO PAGE ONE.

...

Be back in 15 min — Mr. K.

...

LISTEN, NERDS.

SLAM

I GOT PLACES TO BE. SO MY HOMEWORK? MAKE IT HAPPEN.

• AGGRESSION, DOMINANCE

I AM BEST!! BOW TO ME!!

....!

L-LIZARD BRAIN...

....!

...WHAT'D YOU CALL ME?!

U-UH... NOTHING.

I HEARD YOU! YOU CALLED ME A LIZARD BRAIN, YOU...

...FATSO!

YANIC!! THAT'S QUITE ENOUGH!

....!

HE STARTED IT!! HE CALLED ME A LIZARD BRAIN!

YOU ARE DISRUPTING THE GROUP, YANIC...

...AGAIN.

MOVE YOUR THINGS TO MY DESK.

I WILL BE YOUR GROUP.

....!

THIS...FEELS LIKE IT WON'T END WELL.

...

GLARE

123

CHAPTER 6

RRING

THE NEXT DAY.

WHY DOES MATH HAVE TO BE SO HARD...

...AND WHY DOES YANIC HAVE TO BE THERE?

...AT LEAST ENGLISH IS GOING WELL.

RRING

HI, MISS LEE!

GOOD MORNING, JENSEN.

HI, JORGE!

'SUP.

OKAY, EVERYONE, TODAY IS ANOTHER WORK PERIOD FOR YOUR GROUP PRESENTATIONS, SO USE IT WELL!

TAKA TAKA TAK

OUR PRESENTATION IS GOING TO BE SO AWESOME...

...EVEN IF IT'S ALL ABOUT BASEBALL.

WELL, THE HISTORY.

JORGE'S IN CHARGE OF THE WRITTEN PART, AND I'M IN CHARGE OF THE VISUAL AIDS —

125

DRAWINGS OF SOCIALLY HISTORICAL BASEBALL MOMENTS...

...LIKE THE FIRST AFRICAN-AMERICAN PLAYERS, THE FIRST LADY PLAYERS...

LIZZIE ARLINGTON

MOSES FLEETWOOD "FLEET" WALKER

BUD FOWLER

ELIZABETH "LIZZIE" MURPHY

LUIS MANUEL CASTRO

TONI STONE

I DIDN'T KNOW PEOPLE WERE SUCH JERKS TO THEM!

I HAVE TO DRAW THOSE PEOPLE TOO, THE ONES WHO WERE EVIL AND HARASSED THE PLAYERS.

I DON'T LIKE THAT PART.

I'M MAKING THEM LOOK EXTRA EVIL SO THAT NO ONE GETS CONFUSED.

WHOA, HA-HA! THESE ARE *ON POINT.*

THANKS! I'M GONNA ADD COLOR TOO.

DUDE, YOU'RE A REALLY GOOD ARTIST.

...HUH? WHY'S THERE A CROWD HERE?

ARTS FESTIVAL

AUTHORS! CONTESTS! PRIZES!

J.Y. SMITH!

SKYPE

INA CRUZ!

....!

J.Y. SMITH?!

RS! CONTESTS! PRIZES!

J.Y. SMITH!

AT OUR SCHOOL?!

ME TOO!!

NO WAY!

I READ ALL HIS BOOKS!!!

...OH!! THEY FINISHED THE POSTER!

...THE FESTIVAL IS SO SOON!!

J.Y. SMITH...

INA CRUZ...

I STILL DON'T KNOW WHO ALL THOSE AUTHORS ARE.

LUNCH.

LIBRARY

JENSEN... JENSEN...

TAKA TAKA

AH! YOU'RE NEXT ON THE WAITING LIST!

COME BACK IN A COUPLE OF DAYS. WE SHOULD HAVE A FEW COPIES RETURNED BY THEN.

...

YUSSSS.

I'M GOING TO READ ALL THOSE BOOKS...

CAFETERI

RRRRING

...AND WHEN PEOPLE AT ART CLUB TALK ABOUT THEM, I'LL BE ABLE TO JOIN IN!

HEY, GUYS, GUESS WHAT!

WHOA, HEY, WHAT ARE YOU DOING?

HUH...?

SITTING... DOWN?

NO!

I'M SAVING THIS SEAT FOR PEPPI!

SHOO, GO FIND ANOTHER SEAT!

...

BUT...

...THERE ISN'T ANOTHER ONE...

PEPPI'S NOT COMING, TESS!

SHE'S WORKING ON THE "PROJECT" WITH HER "NOT-BOYFRIEND."

UGH, **WHAT**?!

AGAIN?

SO JENSEN CAN SIT THERE, RIGHT?

UGH, I GUESS.

. . .

ANYWAY, GUYS, WHAT'RE YOU MOST EXCITED FOR AT THE FESTIVAL?!

J.Y. SMITH, DUH.

THE ART CONTEST!

NO, NO, GUYS. THE **COSTUME** CONTEST.

WE CAN DRESS UP AGAIN!! IT'S LIKE A SECOND HALLOWEEN!

I KNOW, RIGHT?! NINA AND I ARE GONNA GO AS...

...DISNEY WARRIOR PRINCESSES!

WE'RE GONNA SLAY SO HARD.

OH, WE'LL SEE ABOUT THAT.

I'M GONNA WEAR MY **SAILOR SUNBURST** COSPLAY.

YOUR WHA...?

YEAH, YOU HEARD ME.

THE ONE THAT'S GOT **RIBBONS** FOR THE FIRE EFFECTS.

I'M **SO** GONNA WIN.

131

WH-WHO'S SAILOR SU—

OH, ONLY THE BEST **SAILOR SCOUT** EVER.

HER SPECIAL ATTACK'S A GIANT FIREBALL.

ARE YOU GONNA DRESS UP, JENSEN?

...OH!

UH, YES! I'M GONNA BE—

WAIT, WAIT!

I'M A PSYCHIC AND WILL READ YOUR MIND...

YOU WILL BE...

...AN ASTRONAUT? WITH A CARDBOARD BOX HELMET.

HA HA

UGH, DON'T BE STUPID, NATHANIEL.

HE'S GONNA GO AS A **SUNSPOT**, DUH, DRESSED IN, LIKE, A GARBAGE BAG.

...

HA HA YE OM

HA HA HA

OMG, YES, JENSEN IS A **SUNSPOT**!!

HA HA HA

HE'S TOTALLY BIG ENOUGH TO BLOCK OUT THE SUN ☺

Ha... Ha-ha...

...THIS FEELS WEIRD.

GUYS, STOP BEING **JERKS**.

GEEZ.

HA HA HA HA

BUT IT'S **FUNNY**!

CHILL OUT, FELICITY.

JENSEN, YOU OKAY?

...

Y-YEAH!

YEAH...THEY'RE JUST JOKING.

WELL, DON'T LET 'EM RIDE YOU.

RRRING

...AT LEAST I **THINK** THEY ARE JOKING.

BULLYING CULTURE SURVEY

...

...*"REPEATED CASES OF DISMISSIVE AND MEAN JOKES AT YOUR EXPENSE."*

BUT...

...IT'S OKAY IF THEY'RE MY FRIENDS...

...RIGHT?

. . .

. . .

...I WISH THEY WOULDN'T THOUGH.

...MAKE FUN OF ME LIKE THAT.

HEE HEE HEE

BONK

HA HA

HA HA

FLIP FLIP ...

MONDAY, LUNCH.

H-HI, GUYS...

HEEY, SPACEMAN!

JENSEN!

ARE YOU HERE FOR THE INTERVIEW?

WOW, I DIDN'T EVEN HAVE TO TEXT YOU!

...ALSO, YOU'RE EARLY. WE'RE STILL EATING.

YOU CAN JOIN US!

HERE, GRAB A SEAT.

DID YOU FILL OUT THE SURVEY?

UH, YEAH, I DID.

UM, I...

I HAVE A QUESTION.

YEAH?

THE, UH... "MEAN AND DISMISSIVE JOKES" PART...

IT DOESN'T COUNT IF IT'S FROM *FRIENDS*, RIGHT?

...WHAT?

ARE YOU SERIOUS...?

IT *TOTALLY* COUNTS. IT COUNTS FOR *MORE*, BECAUSE THEY'RE SUPPOSED TO BE YOUR FRIENDS!

...JENSEN, WHA...?

ARE YOUR *FRIENDS* SAYING MEAN THINGS TO YOU TOO?

u-uh...

well...

N-NO!

THEY'RE... THEY'RE JUST JOKING.

. . .

DUDE, UH...

IF THEY SAY MEAN CRAP ABOUT YOU JUST FOR KICKS AND LAUGHS...

...ARE YOU **SURE** THEY'RE YOUR **FRIENDS**?

....!

OKAY, ENOUGH EXPLAINING. WE GOTTA DO THE INTERVIEW— WE'RE SO BEHIND SCHEDULE ALREADY.

...

WHY WOULD HE SAY...

AKILAH, DO YOU HAVE THE QUESTIONS?

FELIPE, MIC HIM UP, PLEASE!

OF...OF COURSE THEY'RE MY FRIENDS!

OVER HERE, JENSEN!

...AREN'T THEY?

•REC

OKAY, THIS IS TAKE TWO!

INTERVIEW WITH JENSEN GRAHAM, STUDY PARTICIPANT TWELVE!

137

JENSEN, YOU JUST MENTIONED THAT EVEN YOUR FRIENDS HARASS YOU.

U-UH.

CAN YOU TELL US HOW THAT AFFECTS YOUR LIFE?

...

...

...

Um, is...

Is this going to be on Berry Scoop?

Will the whole school see —

WHAT? NO, NO!

THIS IS JUST FOR OUR PROJECT.

ONLY OUR TEACHER WILL SEE IT.

...A TEACHER?!

UH, YEAH.

....

UH...

COULD...

...

COULD WE SKIP THAT QUESTION?

I'M NOT...

...JENSEN, ALL THE OTHER QUESTIONS ARE LIKE THIS.

IT'S OUR *TOPIC!*

...O-OH.

...

UH.

...JENSEN, UGH...

I SHOULD'VE ASKED THIS AT THE BEGINNING—

GUH

—ARE YOU OKAY TALKING ABOUT YOUR EXPERIENCES...

...ON *CAMERA?*

·REC

U-UH...

IT'S OKAY TO SAY NO, JENSEN...

...IF YOU'RE NOT OKAY.

...

...

I...

I'M NOT OKAY.

....!

UUUGH

IT'S FINE, IT'S FINE!

STOMP STOMP

D-DID I DO SOMETHING WRONG??

NO, NO, IT'S FINE!

WE'VE HAD OTHER PEOPLE SAY NO TOO!

BANG BANG

IT'S OKAY.

JENNY'S JUST HAVING A LIZARD BRAIN REACTION.

HIGHER FUNCTIONS KICKING IN, IN THREE, TWO, ONE—

...JENNY?

...SORRY FOR FREAKING OUT LIKE THAT!

I WAS JUST A LITTLE FRUSTRATED AT ALL THE WASTED TIME.

BUT CONSENT IS VERY IMPORTANT, SO IF YOU DON'T WANT TO...

...YOU DON'T HAVE TO.

SHAKE

TH-THANK YOU FOR YOUR TIME, JENSEN!

NOW, YOU WON'T **BELIEVE** THE AMOUNT OF WORK WE HAVE TO DO...

...ARTICLES TO WRITE, VIDEOS TO EDIT...**OODLES** OF WORK!

PUSH

SO PLEASE GO AHEAD AND ENJOY THE REST OF YOUR LUNCH WHILE WE GET TO THAT.

BYE, JENSEN!

COME BY FOR LUNCH AGAIN SOMETIME!

YEAH. BYE.

KTK

...I FEEL LIKE I DID SOMETHING WRONG.

UUGH!!!!

CAN YOU BELIEVE HIM?

....!

...YEP, DEFINITELY DID SOMETHING WRONG...

CAFETERIA

PEEK ... ...THERE'S THE ART CLUB.

HA HA YAMMER

...THE ONLY EMPTY SEAT IS BY TESSA...

I'M SAVING IT FOR PEPPI!

IT'S PROBABLY TAKEN...

...I'M JUST...GONNA GO O-OUTSIDE.

MAYBE I SHOULD TRY TO READ MORE OF JENNY AND AKILAH'S PAPER.

MAYBE THEN JENNY WILL BE LESS UPSET...

...WHAT IS THIS CULTURE STUFF?

"BEHAVIORAL CULTURE IS A SET OF ATTITUDES AND ACCEPTED BEHAVIOR IN A SOCIAL GROUP.

...

"IT BUILDS OVER TIME, ACTION BY ACTION, LIKE BRICK BY BRICK.

...OH, THERE'RE CARTOONS AGAIN...

"FOR EXAMPLE, EACH TIME PEOPLE THROW GARBAGE ON THE GROUND INSTEAD OF INTO A GARBAGE CAN...

"...THEY HELP BUILD A CULTURE WHERE LITTERING IS NORMALIZED AND ACCEPTED."

garbage everywhere is just how things are! everyone does it.

YEP.

...OOPS, I DO THAT.

S-SOMETIMES.

"ON THE OTHER HAND, EVERY TIME A PERSON DOESN'T LITTER, OR PICKS IT UP, OR EVEN PREVENTS IT...

"...LITTLE BY LITTLE, ACTION 'BRICK' BY ACTION 'BRICK,' THEY HELP BUILD A BEHAVIORAL CULTURE WHERE LITTERING IS *NOT* THE NORM.

"THROUGHOUT HUMAN HISTORY, EXISTING BEHAVIORAL CULTURES WERE CHALLENGED, DISMANTLED, AND NEW ONES BUILT FROM SCRATCH.

"ANYONE CAN TRY TO BUILD A CULTURE; ON A SOCIETY-WIDE SCALE, AFFECTING AN ENTIRE NATION...

"...OR EVEN ON A MUCH SMALLER SCALE, LIKE WITHIN A SINGLE FAMILY OR JUST ONE SCHOOL."

...!

...e smaller scale
...e school.

SURVEY QUESTION:

What culture would **YOU** want to build? What would be the norm there?

Which actions would help build this culture?

WHAT...

...CULTURE...?

...

HA HA

...

MAYBE...

...ONE...WHERE I DON'T HAVE TO...

...EAT LUNCH ALONE?

CHAPTER 7

RRING

BERRYBROOK MIDDLE SCHOOL

THE NEXT DAY.

...MY HEAD IS SWIMMING. CULTURES...? LIZARD BRAINS...?

WHY IS MIDDLE SCHOOL SO COMPLICATED...?

JENSEN, PAY ATTENTION!

IS ATTENTION A LIZARD BRAIN THING?

OR A HIGHER FUNCTION THING?

JENSEN, WAKE UP!!

I MISS JUST BEING A KID. A HUMAN ONE.

...I WONDER WHO ELSE AKILAH AND JENNY INTERVIEWED.

I WAS NUMBER TWELVE... WHO ARE THE OTHER ELEVEN?

...I BET IT WASN'T **THEM**.

HEE HEE

HEE

SLINK SLINK

BTW, I **LOVE** THAT DRESS!

AWW, THANKS!

IT LOOKS JUST LIKE MY GRANDMA'S CURTAINS!

...

...SHE THREW THEM OUT RECENTLY, SAID THEY WERE TOO '80S.

. . .

HA HA

HA

HA

HA

I'M **SO** GLAD YOU RESCUED THEM FROM THE TRASH.

Shrink

WHA...?

H-ha.

Ha ha...

That's funny...

YOU'RE ALWAYS SUCH A JOKER, JO!

THAT...

THAT WAS LIKE WHAT TESSA AND NATHANIEL DO TO ME!

RRING

just one school. ...*aller* scale,

SURVEY QUESTION:

What culture would **YOU** want to build? What would be the norm there?

Which actions would help build this culture?

WHAT KIND OF CULTURE...?

WHERE IT'S NOT OKAY TO BE MEAN TO YOUR FRIENDS!

AND...AND WHERE PEOPLE SAVE A SEAT FOR ME AT LUNCH.

"...WHAT ACTIONS WOULD HELP BUILD THIS CULTURE?"

...

UH...

HMM.

OH!

MAYBE...

PSST.

PENELOPE?

HMM?

U-UM, I'M GOING TO BE LATE FOR LUNCH, AND, UH...

C-COULD...

COULD YOU SAVE ME A SEAT?

...AT THE ART CLUB TABLE?

OH!

ACTUALLY, JAIME AND I ARE STILL WORKING ON THAT PROJECT...

...SO I WON'T BE THERE.

OH.

BUT YOU CAN ASK TESSA!

RRING

...WELL, THAT DIDN'T WORK.

WHAT ELSE CAN I DO?

...THE TABLE IS FULL AGAIN.

THERE'RE EVEN KIDS FROM THE SCIENCE CLUB?!

...

MAYBE...

...THEY'LL MAKE ROOM FOR ME?

IF I ASK...?

HA HA

...I'M AFRAID TO ASK...

LIBRARY

JENSEN!

...!

I WAS JUST ABOUT TO PING YOU!

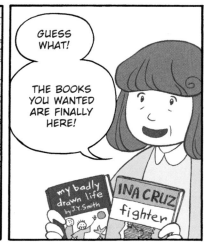

GUESS WHAT!

THE BOOKS YOU WANTED ARE FINALLY HERE!

my badly drawn life by J.Y.Smith

INA CRUZ fighter

.....!!

WOULD YOU LIKE TO SIGN THEM OUT?

YES!

OH WOW, OH WOW.

I BETTER START WITH J.Y. SMITH —THAT'S THE ONE EVERYONE'S TALKING ABOUT.

BZZ

PING

....!

A TEXT?

...FROM PEPPI!

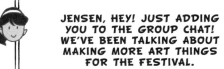

JENSEN, HEY! JUST ADDING YOU TO THE GROUP CHAT! WE'VE BEEN TALKING ABOUT MAKING MORE ART THINGS FOR THE FESTIVAL.

LOOKS LIKE TESSA FORGOT TO ADD YOU, OOPS.

(STOP DOING THAT, TESS! HA-HA!)

...SHE FORGOT TO ADD ME. AGAIN.

BZZ PING!
BZZ PING!
BZZ PING!

WHATEVER ⊖ STOP BEING SO FORGETTABLE, JENSEN!

TESS, UGH.

WHAAAAT! IT'S TRUE!

every1 forgets jensen

EVEN HIS MOM

BZZ PING
BZZ PING

I'M NOT...

...FORGETTABLE...

153

PUSH

HAPPY READING, BOOKWORM.

HA HA

. . .

HA HA

...IF I'M SO FORGETTABLE, WHY WON'T **THEY** FORGET ABOUT ME??

MATH TUTORING.

SIGH

. . .

YOU OKAY, JENSEN?

um.

. . .

...WHAT DO YOU THINK ABOUT THE BULLYING CULTURE AT BERRYBROOK?

. . . . !

...Y-YEAH.

WHAT DO YOU THINK ABOUT THAT LIZARD BRAIN STUFF?

EH.

HAHA HA

DID JENNY AND AKILAH ROPE YOU INTO THEIR PROJECT TOO?

I DUNNO ABOUT THAT.

GOOD PEOPLE SOMETIMES DO BAD THINGS, AND BAD PEOPLE DO GOOD THINGS...IT'S COMPLICATED.

NOD NOD

...I LIKE THE STUFF ABOUT CHANGING CULTURE THOUGH.

FIXING WHAT DOESN'T WORK...

...I'D BE GAME FOR THAT.

...

...AARON'S SO SMART.

HIM AND VICKIE BOTH.

(TURNS OUT SHE'S HERE BECAUSE THEY'RE PRACTICING FOR A MATH COMPETITION!!)

...ME, I STILL CAN'T DO MY MATH HOMEWORK WITHOUT HELP...

...OR READ THAT LIZARD BRAIN PAPER.

WHAT IF...

WHAT IF I **AM** STUPID? LIKE PEOPLE SAY?

MAYBE I SHOULDN'T EVEN TRY...

...TO BE A NASA ASTRONAUT...

THE NEXT DAY.

HA HA HA

SHOVE

HA HA HA

HE'S SO FAT, HE CAN'T EVEN FIT, HA-HA!

...

HA HA

...

LUNCH.

HA HA HA

THE TABLE IS FULL AGAIN.

...WHY DO PEOPLE LIKE THIS BOOK...?

THE MAIN CHARACTER IS A JERK.

HE KEEPS DOING MEAN THINGS TO PEOPLE AND SAYING IT'S A JOKE.

"WITH FRIENDS LIKE YOU, WHO NEEDS ENEMIES!!"

....

THE NEXT DAY.

I WILL NOW RETURN YOUR QUIZ RESULTS!

JENSEN.

ONLY A "D"...?

I THOUGHT I'D DO BETTER, AFTER TUTORING...

...

...SO MUCH FOR BEING A NASA ASTRONAUT.

RRRING

LUNCH.

...I SHOULD CHECK WITH THE NEWSPAPER. MAYBE THEY NEED HELP!

JENSEN!

UH...

NOW'S ACTUALLY NOT A GOOD TIME...

WE'RE **SWAMPED**. SORRY...

AKILAH, ARE YOU DONE DRAF—

MY DRAMA CLUB ARTICLE GOT PULLED! SO NOW, WE HAVE TO FILL A CONTENT HOLE...

...AND **NO** ONE'S SUBMITTED **ANY**THING FOR THE SUBMISSIONS CALL...

O-OH.

GOOD LUCK!

THANKS, JENSEN!

BYE!

KTK

CAFETERIA

...JENNY HASN'T TEXTED ME IN SEVERAL DAYS...SHE'S EITHER STILL MAD AT ME...

...OR THEY DON'T NEED ME.

...

...DOES ANYONE NEED ME?

...

RRSTLE

BRR

...IT'S COLD TODAY.

...SHOULD I...

...WORK ON SOMETHING...?

ALL RIGHT, TEN PUSHUPS AND TEN JUMPING JACKS.

cough cough cough

EEW, JENSEN, STOP SPREADING YOUR GERMS!

HA HA

EVACUATE THE AREA!

JENSEN, ARE YOU OKAY?

YOU DON'T LOOK SO GOOD.

COUGH

MBLL

WOBBLE

GUIDANCE/ NURSE

...RIGHT. HOW ABOUT WE GET YOU TO THE NURSE'S OFFICE?

OH YEAH, YOU'RE DEFINITELY BURNING UP.

LOOKS LIKE IT'S A FLU. I'M GOING TO RECOMMEND THAT YOU STAY HOME FOR A FEW DAYS.

SHIVER

I'LL BE CALLING YOUR MOTHER TO COME GET YOU.

IS THERE A FRIEND YOU WANT TO PICK UP YOUR HOMEWORK WHILE YOU'RE OUT SICK?

...

I DON'T...

...HAVE...

...A FRIEND...

my head is so hot and achy...

it feels like i have ebola or something...

CHAPTER 8

A WEEK LATER.

...IT WAS JUST A FLU, AFTER ALL...

...OR SO THE DOCTOR CLAIMS.

I TRIED TO GET THEM TO RUN MORE TESTS, BUT...

...THEY SAID IT'S TIME TO GO BACK.

RRING

EVERYTHING IS THE SAME. IT'S LIKE I NEVER LEFT...

(SO IF I START A ZOMBIE EPIDEMIC, IT'LL BE THEIR FAULT.)

...EXCEPT I MISSED THE ARTS FESTIVAL.

...I LOST FOUR POUNDS WHILE SICK THOUGH.

MAYBE NOW PEOPLE WON'T CALL ME FAT?

SHOVE

FATSO, YOU'RE BACK!

...OR NOT.

HA HA HA HA HA

HAVE YOU GUYS SEEN FELICITY?

IS SHE BACK?

....?

I DON'T THINK SO...

FELICITY?

ART CLUB FELICITY?

....!

JUSTICE 4 FELICITY!!

BRING HER BACK!!!

...IT IS HER!

WHAAA...

...WHAT DID I MISS *NOW*?

JUSTICE 4 FELICITY!!

BRING HER BACK!!!

ENGLISH.

JENSEN!

YOU'RE BACK!

ARE YOU FEELING BETTER?

U-UH, YEAH, A LOT BETTER!

THANKS.

WHAT'S THAT ABOUT FELICITY?

I SAW THE FLYERS.

UGH, IT'S SO *UNFAIR* WHAT THEY DID, JENSEN!!

WH-WHAT HAPPENED?

SO, REMEMBER SHE WAS GOING TO DRESS UP FOR THE ARTS FESTIVAL?

AS SAILOR SUNBURST, THAT ANIME CHARACTER?

169

...JORGE, PLEASE START BY EXPLAINING YOUR COMMENT ON MISS TEALE'S SUSPENSION.

...UH, I DON'T MEAN TO BE DISRESPECTFUL, MISS LEE, BUT...THEY'RE MAKING HER MISS *CLASSES*...

...OVER A *SKIRT.*

WOW, I'VE NEVER SEEN MISS LEE SO ANGRY.

TRUE. THE SCHOOL ADMIN DECIDED THAT A GIRL'S *CLOTHES* WERE MORE IMPORTANT THAN HER *EDUCATION*.

CLASS, WHAT ARE YOUR THOUGHTS ON THIS?

WELL, SHE DID BREAK THE RULES, MISS LEE.

SHE SHOULD'VE WORN A LONGER SKIRT.

ALSO TRUE. SHE COULD'VE WORN A LONGER SKIRT.

HOW LONG A SKIRT, DO YOU THINK?

...

I DUNNO.

LIKE, KNEE-LENGTH?

...

EVOLUTION OF CIVIL LIBERTIES: THEN AND NOW.

SKRT

ALL RIGHT, I WANT EVERYONE TO WRITE DOWN SOME DISCUSSION POINTS AND THEN BREAK UP INTO GROUPS.

RRRRING

YAMMER

WOW, MISS LEE WAS INTENSE TODAY.

YEAH. I DIDN'T KNOW ABOUT ALL THAT STUFF.

...THAT DOESN'T HELP US GET FELICITY BACK THOUGH!

WE'VE *GOT* TO COME UP WITH SOME WAY.

ART CLUB IS MEETING OUTSIDE FOR LUNCH TODAY— WE'RE GONNA BRAINSTORM IDEAS AGAIN.

ARE YOU COMING? WANT ME TO SAVE YOU A SPOT?

Y-YES!

YES, PLEASE!

GREAT, I'LL SEE YOU THERE!

WOW.

...PEPPI'S REALLY NICE.

JUSTICE 4 FELICITY!!

BRING HER BACK!!!

...

...WAIT.

I THINK I KNOW WHO CAN HELP!

LUNCH.

THE NEWSPAPER CREW! THEY'RE THE JUSTICE SQUAD! THEY'RE ALL ABOUT THIS STUFF!

HEEEY, SPACEMAN!

FELIPE!

ARE JENNY AND AKILAH HERE?

I HAVE TO TELL THEM—

UH.

MAAAYBE NOT A GOOD TIME?

TAK TAK TAK

W-WOW... WHAT'S WRONG?

. . .

WHAT DO YOU WANT, JENSEN?

U-UH... FELICITY... SUSPENDED... ...HELP...?

OH, DON'T ASK *HER* FOR HELP, JENSEN.

I'VE BEEN OVER THIS WITH MISS OH-NO ALREADY.

UGH, NOT THIS AGAIN.

SHE'D RATHER SWEEP IT UNDER A *RUG* THAN *REPORT* ON IT.

LOOK.

EVEN IF WE WROTE THE ARTICLE, THEY WOULD NEVER LET US PUBLISH IT!

YOU DON'T KNOW THAT! NOT IF YOU DON'T EVEN TRY!

I DO KNOW THAT! I KNOW EXACTLY WHAT'LL HAPPEN!!

THE SAME THING THAT HAPPENED WITH YOUR STUPID DRAMA CLUB ARTICLE!

177

...MY "STUPID"...?!

RRSTL

WE SPENT ALL THAT TIME! ENERGY! AND WHAT DID THEY SAY?!

"THIS MATTER IS BEST HANDLED AS AN INTERNAL INVESTIGATION. PLEASE FOLLOW SCHOOL RULES, OR YOUR CLUB WILL BE SUSPENDED."

SUSPENDED, AKILAH!

THEY COULD SHUT DOWN THE NEWSPAPER!

THEY ALREADY *HAVE!!*

THEY KEEP SHUTTING DOWN ALL THE *REAL STORIES!!*

DO YOU WANT TO KEEP WRITING USELESS ARTICLES AND HALLWAY GOSSIP?

USELESS?! SOME PEOPLE LIKE READING HALLWAY GOSSIP! NOT EVERYONE'S A SNOBBY ELITE JOURNALIST WANNABE!

AND IF YOU'D JUST STOP BEING STUPID AND STUBBORN ABOUT—

......!!

...Y-YOU KNOW WHAT?

HOW ABOUT I STOP BEING HERE, *PERIOD*.

IF YOU WANT TO KEEP RUNNING USELESS CRAP, YOU *DO* THAT.

....!

I QUIT.

...

...

o-oh yeah?

well...

well, FINE!

...i

I DON'T NEED YOU!

I DON'T NEED ANY OF YOU!!!

EVERYONE, GET OUT!! D-DON'T COME BACK!!

WH-WHAT JUST HAPPENED?

WAS THAT A FRIEND-FIGHT...?

NOOOPE.

THAT WAS A REAL FIGHT.

...I'M JUST...

...GONNA GO. AND NOT COME BACK FOR A WHILE.

...

CAFETERIA

JENSEN, THERE YOU ARE!

PEPPI DID SAVE ME A SEAT!

OVER HERE, COME SIT!

OKAY, SO HERE'S THE IDEA LIST SO FAR—

CHEW CHEW

FLIP FLIP

...

...JENSEN!

HUH?

DO *YOU* HAVE ANY IDEAS?

WE SHOUL TALK TO T PRINCIPAL

ARE YO SERIOU

U-UH...

I'M THINKING...?

...WELL, HOW ABOUT PUTTING UP MORE FLYERS?

THAT DID **NOTHING!**

...

CAN WE DO A FUND-RAISER?

FOR **WHAT**?

...IF EVEN THE NEWSPAPER CAN'T HELP...

...WHAT CAN ANYONE DO?

. . .

CHAPTER 9

THE NEXT DAY.

MATH TUTORING WAS SO HARD YESTERDAY.

ISN'T IT SUPPOSED TO GET EASIER?

JUSTICE 4 FELICITY!!

BRING HER BACK!!!

...

...FELICITY'S STILL NOT BACK...

...

...AND THE NEWSPAPER CREW IS STILL BROKEN.

MATH.

SIGH...

ALL RIGHT, CLASS DISMISSED!

AS YOU LEAVE, PICK UP THESE PRACTICE PROBLEMS FOR NEXT WEEK'S TEST!

JENSEN.

Y-YES?

AARON TELLS ME YOU ARE MAKING PROGRESS IN TUTORING.

GOOD JOB.

....! R-REALLY?

BUT...

...I STILL DON'T UNDERSTAND EVEN HALF OF IT...

YOU'RE JUST VERY BEHIND, JENSEN. THAT'S ALL.

IT'LL TAKE TIME AND HARD WORK, BUT YOU'LL CATCH UP.

JUST KEEP GOING AND DON'T QUIT.

...HUH.

MAYBE HE'S NOT THAT EVIL, AFTER ALL.

CAFETERIA

...I HOPE THERE'S A SPOT AT THE ART TABLE. BET THEY'RE STILL TRYING TO HELP FELICITY...

...I STILL DON'T HAVE A SINGLE IDEA FOR THAT.

....!

FOSTER AND YANIC!!

...PHEW, THEY DIDN'T SEE ME.

HA HA

...BETTER KEEP IT THAT WAY.

...I THINK I'LL JUST EAT OUTSIDE.

I CAN BRAINSTORM SOME IDEAS ON HOW TO HELP FELICITY!

...

...AKILAH.

...SH-SHOULD I MAKE SURE SHE'S OKAY?

OR DOES SHE WANT TO BE LEFT ALONE...?

...I-I'LL ASK.

IF SHE WANTS ME TO LEAVE, I WILL.

H-HI, AKILAH!

...

IS THIS SPOT TAKEN?

...

UM... NO.

...

...H-HOW ARE YOU?

....!

...

FINE.

SHE DOESN'T LOOK FINE.

...I'M NO GOOD AT THIS... I DON'T KNOW WHAT TO SAY.

U-UH.

IT'S SURE WEIRD TO SEE YOU WITHOUT JENNY.

...OOPS. SHOULD I HAVE SAID THAT?! I DON'T—

...

IT IS WEIRD.

WE'VE ALWAYS HUNG OUT TOGETHER.

SINCE KINDERGARTEN!

WOW, YOU MET IN KINDERGARTEN?

...

YEAH. WE WERE, LIKE, FIVE?

THESE TWO BIGGER KIDS WERE HARASSING ME...

191

SNFFLE

....

A-ARE...
...ARE YOU OKAY?

NO!

I MISS MY BEST FRIEND!

I HATE THAT WE HAD THAT HUGE FIGHT!

....

...

M-MAYBE YOU'LL MAKE UP?

MAYBE IT'S JUST...

...LIZARD BRAIN STUFF?

....

...!

...WHAT?!

THAT HAS NOTHING TO DO WITH—

...WAIT.

...WE WERE ANGRY. AND HURT.

...SO WE LASHED OUT...

...INSTEAD OF PROBLEM SOLVING.

...IT TOTALLY **WAS.**

IT WAS A LIZARD BRAIN REACTION.

...

C'MON, JENSEN!!

....?

IT'S NOT TOO LATE TO FIX THIS!

NEWSPAPER
OFFICE

JENNY?

WE GOTTA TALK!

APER
ICE

Akilah?

Wha—

What do you want?

...JENNY...

...ARE YOU CRYING?

NO!!

WHY ARE YOU GUYS HERE?!!

NEWSPAPER OFFICE

I...

I CAME TO APOLOGIZE...

...FOR... FOR JUST WALKING OUT LIKE THAT...

...FOR SAYING THE STUFF I SAID.

....!

...I'M *SORRY*.

DO YOU WANNA BE FRIENDS AGAIN?

OH MY GOD, I'M THE ONE WHO'S SORRY!!

I SAID TERRIBLE STUFF TO YOU!!

I'M SO GLAD YOU'RE BACK!!

I PROMISE I WON'T BE A JERK ANYMORE!!

POKE

HEEEY.

FRIENDS AGAIN?

TO THE END OF THE WORLD!

IS IT SAFE TO COME BACK?

...OH GOOD, YOU GUYS ALL MADE UP.

LISTEN, WE **REALLY** GOTTA FIGURE SOMETHING OUT FOR FELICITY. IT'S NOT FAIR.

YES!!

WE'RE BACK, AND WE'RE GONNA DO THIS!!

I'VE BEEN RACKING MY BRAIN ON THIS... WHAT CAN WE EVEN DO?

WE CAN'T PUT ANYTHING IN THE PAPER...

CAN WE TRY TO SNEAK IT INTO BERRY SCOOP?

...NOOOO, THAT'S MONITORED BY THE SCHOOL ADMIN TOO.

SNORE

...I WAS THINKING— WHAT IF WE START A PETITION?

GET STUDENTS AND TEACHERS TO SIGN IT, THEN TAKE IT TO THE SCHOOL BOARD?

THEY MIGHT TAKE THAT MORE SERIOUSLY.

....!

OMG YES

THAT'S EXACTLY WHAT WE WILL DO!!

...WE HAVE A PLAN?

THE NEXT DAY.

ALL RIGHT, EVERYONE, HERE IT IS, FRESH OFF THE PRINTER!

PETITION: BRING BACK FELICITY!!!

ADD YOUR NAME TO JOIN THE RIGHT SIDE OF HISTORY! WE ARE PETITIONING TO:

*LIFT FELICITY'S SUSPENSION!!

*UPDATE THE SCHOOL DRESS CODE FROM THE 18TH CENTURY TO THE 21ST!

name	class
11	
12	
13	
14	

name	class

BERRYBROO

ART CLUB!

SCIENCE CLUB!

EVERYONE ELSE!

WE NEED **ONE HUNDRED** SIGNATURES...

...BY THE END OF **TODAY!**

WE HAVE A PLAN!

SO, EACH ONE OF YOU—TAKE A SHEET AND GET AS MANY SIGNATURES AS YOU CAN BY THE LAST BELL!

BRING THEM BACK HERE, AND WE'LL COLLECT THEM FOR THE MEETING.

DO **NOT** BE LATE!

RRRNG

...I GOTTA GET **LOTS** OF SIGNATURES.

...H-HOW ARE WE SUPPOSED TO DO THIS?

DO YOU THINK IT'S FAIR THAT YOU CAN GET SUSPENDED OVER A **SKIRT**?

WHAT?! **NO!**

THEN YOU SHOULD SIGN OUR PETITION!

OHHH.

...DO YOU THINK IT'S FAIR THAT—

UH.

PASS.

O-OKAY.

...WOULD YOU LIKE TO SIGN—

UGH, WHAT? LEAVE ME ALONE.

OOOKAY...THIS IS HARDER THAN IT LOOKED.

HEY!

HEY, YOU!

WEIRD GUY! YES, *YOU!*

COME OVER HERE!

IS THAT THE PETITION?

U-UH, YES...

GIMME.

SNATCH

WH-WHAT IS SHE GONNA...?

YOU'RE SIGNING IT?

YES! AND YOU SHOULD TOO!

SCRIBBLL

THE DRESS RULES ARE STUPID— LIZ GOT IN TROUBLE FOR *LEGGINGS!*

THEY'D MAKE US WEAR POTATO SACKS IF THEY COULD!

HERE, GUY.

SHOVE

LET'S GO.

....!

...I GOT MY FIRST SIGNATURE!

SEVERAL HOURS LATER.

THIS IS EXHAUSTING...

I'VE ASKED SO MANY PEOPLE...

...BUT ONLY GOT THREE SIGNATURES.

I HOPE OTHERS ARE HAVING BETTER LUCK.

GAH!

SNATCH

HEY, FATSO, WHATCHA GOT THERE?

OH, LOOK, IT'S A PETIIIIITION!

H-HEY

HA

WITH ONLY THREE PEOPLE WHO CARE!

HA

H-HEY!!!

....!

P-PLEASE GIVE THAT BACK!

I NEED THAT!

CRMPLE

PWEESE GIVE THAT BACK, WEH-WEH-WEH!

OH, WHOOPS!

IT'S GARBAGE NOW!

HAHAHA

....!

UGH!!

...WE NEED THOSE SIGNATURES!

rummage rummage

WHY'S HE DIGGING IN THE TRASH?

EEW, GROSS.

MUST... FIND...FOR FELICITY...

THIS IS SO EMBARRASSING...

GOT IT!!

...JENSEN?

HEY, BUDDY, IS EVERYTHING OKAY?

JORGE!

OLIVIA!

...D-DO YOU GUYS WANT TO SIGN OUR PETITION?

RRING

DASH

...JORGE AND OLIVIA DIDN'T JUST SIGN THE PETITION...

...THEY GOT THEIR ENTIRE ATHLETICS CLUB TO SIGN IT TOO!!

I'VE GOT TWENTY-SIX SIGNATURES!!

HERE THEY ARE!

JENSEN!! FINALLY!

YOU'RE THE LAST ONE!

...WHY'S IT ALL CRUMPLED?

...OH, WOW, TWENTY-SIX?! NOW WE DEFINITELY HAVE ENOUGH!!

IS EVERYONE READY TO GO HERE?

WE NEED TO CATCH THE PRINCIPAL BEFORE HE LEAVES.

MISS LEE!

HE WON'T LEAVE. I TOLD PHIL TO HOLD HIM AS LONG AS IT TAKES.

WE'RE GETTING THIS BALL ROLLING *TODAY*.

AGREED.

....!

AND MISS TOBINS! AND MR. KRISTOFFER?!!

...EVEN THE TEACHERS ARE GETTING INVOLVED?!

WE HAVE ALL THE SIGNATURES! READY TO ROLL!

GREAT, LET'S GO!

...DOES THAT MEAN ME TOO?

....!

JENSEN?

WHY AREN'T YOU AT TUTORING?

....!

OR NOT.

IS THIS ENOUGH? 112 SIGNATURES, THAT'S TONS.

TUTORING.

CLICK CLICK CLICK

...I'M ON PINS AND NEEDLES.

WILL THEY GET FELICITY BACK?!

HEY!

STOP CLICKING THAT PEN! IT'S **ANNOYING.**

...OH YEAH, YANIC IS HERE AGAIN.

...

...ARE YOU NERVOUS ABOUT YOUR LITTLE PETITION THAT NO ONE CARES ABOUT?

...

...

BET THEY'RE BEING TOLD TO TAKE A HIKE **RIGHT NOW.**

HA!

...IS IT JUST ME, OR IS YANIC GETTING WORSE...?

I MEAN, HE WAS NEVER AWESOME...

...BUT IT'S LIKE HE'S EXTRA EVIL LATELY.

MUST...NOT...

...LET HIM GET TO ME...

HA H H HA

CHAPTER 10

THE NEXT DAY.

HOMEROOM.

RRRING

H-HOW DID IT GO YESTERDAY?

UH... GOOD?

I THINK?

...THE PRINCIPAL SAID THEY WILL "REVIEW" IT IN A "TIMELY MANNER"!

WHATEVER THAT MEANS.

I THOUGHT FELICITY WOULD BE BACK BY NOW.

RRSTLE BEEP

ATTENTION, STUDENTS.

THIS IS YOUR PRINCIPAL SPEAKING.

CLICK

...

...THAT'S IT?

WHAT ABOUT FELICITY?

I GUESS THEY...WANT TO UPDATE THE DRESS CODE... FIRST?

UGH.

I'M JUST GOING TO WRITE **"BRING BACK FELICITY"** ALL OVER THEIR STUPID QUESTIONNAIRE.

BZZ

PING!

...A TEXT?

BZZ

...?

BZZ

HEY, I GOT A TEXT.

...FROM FELICITY!

IT'S TO THE WHOLE GROUP.

GUYS GUYS WHAAAAT

THEY JUST CALLED MY MOM

...SHE'S STILL TYPING.

○○○

....

...THEY LIFTED THE SUSPENSION?!

YUS!!

WHAT?! OMG!!

IT DID WORK!! IT WORKED!!

SHE'S BACK!!!

AAAAAA

...IT WORKED!

THE NEXT DAY.

WHAT'S UP YOU JERKS ♡

FELICITY!!

WELCOME BACK!!

WE MISSED YOOOOU!!

HUGGS

YOU'RE WEARING A SKIRT!!

YESSS. GONNA GO UP TO THE ADMIN AND BE ALL "SUSPEND *THIS*"!

...I CAN'T BELIEVE YOU GUYS DID THAT WHOLE PETITION THING FOR ME!

HOW DID YOU EVEN...?

BELIEVE IT, LADY!

WE WENT ALL OVER THE WHOLE SCHOOL!

EVEN JENSEN—

HOW MANY SIGNATURES DID YOU GET, JENSEN?

211

T-TWENTY-SIX.

TWENTY-SIX ??!

AWW, C'MERE.

BEAR HUG

THANKS, BUDDY.

MAN, IT'S GOOD TO BE BACK. SO WHAT DID I MISS?

AUGH, SO MUCH DRAMA. HA-HA!

...I'VE NEVER GOTTEN HUGGED BEFORE.
(EXCEPT FROM FAMILY)

I GUESS MIDDLE SCHOOL LIFE CAN BE GOOD, AFTER ALL.

RRING

BERRYBROOK MIDDLE SC

FELICITY BEING BACK WAS HUGE NEWS THAT ENTIRE WEEK.

THE DRESS CODE UPDATE TOO...BIG DRAMA.

A FIVE-INCH SKIRT IS NOT A SKIRT! IT'S A BELT!!

WHY ARE YOU SUCH A PRUDE?!

AKILAH AND JENNY LOVED IT.

BICKER ARGUE

AHHH, THE SWEET, SWEET SOUND OF DEMOCRACY AT WORK...

WE ARE COLLECTING FEEDBACK TO FEATURE ON BERRY SCOOP— WOULD YOU GUYS LIKE TO COMMENT ON RECORD?

fight! fight!

WOULD I?!!

ME TOO!!

...BUT THEN, OLIVIA BROKE UP WITH SEAN, RIGHT IN THE MIDDLE OF THE CAFETERIA.

L-LIV, C'MON, HE'S NOT WORTH IT.

I SAW YOUR TEXTS TO MICHELLE, YOU JERK!!!

DUDE, **RUN**.

RUN **NOW**.

COME OVER HERE AND **FIGHT** ME!!!

OLIVIA TAKES JIUJITSU **AND** KARATE.

...EVERYONE WAS VERY SURPRISED BECAUSE WE ALL THOUGHT SHE WAS DATING JORGE.

did you hear?!

omg i was so surprised!!

...AND THEN, END-OF-THE-YEAR PROJECT DUE DATES AND TESTS CAME...

FIFTY PROBLEMS BY THE END OF THE WEEK!

...AND EVERYONE BECAME TOO BUSY TRYING **NOT TO FAIL** TO GOSSIP ABOUT **ANYTHING**.

GROAN

UUUGH

WHYEEe

SO NOW, EVERYTHING IS PRETTY MUCH BACK TO NORMAL...

...INCLUDING...

GLANCE

LOOK

....!

THERE HE IS!

ACTUALLY, FOSTER AND YANIC DIDN'T JUST GET BACK TO NORMAL...

DASH

...THEY GOT **WORSE.**

DID I LOSE THEM?

I USED TO BE ABLE TO AVOID THEM, BUT NOW...

....IT'S LIKE THEY'RE EVERYWHERE.

IN THE CAFETERIA...

HA HA HA

hey, look, i'm jensen!

HA HA HA

IN THE HALLWAYS BETWEEN CLASSES...

THEY'RE AT MY LOCKER AGAIN!

SOMETIMES EVEN AFTER MATH TUTORING!

....!

U-UM, C-CAN I WALK WITH YOU GUYS?

UH.

SURE.

AND THEY'RE **REALLY SNEAKY.**

THEY NEVER DO IT IN FRONT OF ADULTS, OR EVEN JORGE AND OLIVIA...

'SUP, JENSEN.

H-HI.

...

fat and stupid

...SO I CAN'T PROVE ANYTHING.

...I DON'T KNOW WHAT TO DO.

NEWSPAPER OFFICE.

....!!

....!!

YOU SHOULD **REPORT** THEM, JENSEN!!!

IT'S OBVIOUS THEY'RE **TARGETING** YOU!!!

TELL A TEACHER! A SCHOOL COUNSELOR! ANY ADULT!!

ISN'T...ISN'T THAT SNITCHING?

...WHAT?! NO!!

IT'S SELF-DEFENSE! THEY'RE POISONING YOUR LIFE!

IT'S LIKE— IF THERE WERE TWO *VENOMOUS SNAKES* AFTER YOU, YOU NEED TO REPORT THEM TO PEST CONTROL!

OH.

...

I-I GUESS...

JENSEN, THERE'S...

THERE'S LOTS OF INFO ABOUT THIS— HOW TO DEAL WITH BULLYING...

UUUGH you guess?!

THERE'RE TONS OF SITES...

...AND EVERY SCHOOL COUNSELING OFFICE HAS THESE INFO BOOKLETS.

IT HAS LINKS, FACTS, ADVICE.

...ALSO...

...THERE *IS* SOMETHING YOU COULD TRY...

...TO STOP FOSTER AND YANIC.

IT'S KINDA DANGEROUS...

...BECAUSE I'M NOT SURE IT'LL EVEN WORK ON THEM, BUT...

...DO YOU WANNA HEAR IT?

THE NEXT DAY.

RRING

BERRYBROOK MIDDLE SCHOOL

MATH TUTORING.

OKAY, I THINK THAT'S IT FOR TODAY.

DO YOU HAVE ANY MORE QUESTIONS, JENSEN?

U-UH, NO.

I THINK I GET IT.

YOU'RE GETTING A LOT BETTER, JENSEN!

....!

THANKS, VICKIE.

DID YOU WANT TO WALK WITH US AGAIN?

...

UM.

...TH-THANKS, BUT I GOTTA GET SOMETHING FROM MY LOCKER.

...I DON'T REALLY HAVE TO GET ANYTHING FROM MY LOCKER.

I'M GOING TO...

...DO THE THING...

...AKILAH TOLD ME ABOUT.

...I'VE NEVER BEEN SO SCARED IN MY LIFE.

PEEK

I DON'T SEE THEM...

...ANYWHERE...

MAYBE...

...THEY ALREADY WENT HOME?

KTK

THEN I WOULDN'T...HAVE TO DO THIS.

HEY LOOK, THERE HE IS!

...

CRAP.

I WAS STARTING TO THINK YOU WERE AVOIDING US, JENSEN!

I WAS *HURT!*

HE WAS *SO* HURT.

OH GOD.

STAY CALM, STAY CALM.

...

...

HOW'D TUTORING GO?

YOU STILL DUMB AS A BAG OF ROCKS?

D-DON'T PANIC...

YOU CAN DO THIS.

...IS IT ME, OR IS HE EVEN FATTER TODAY?

...

...

MUST BE THAT BURGER HE HAD FOR LUNCH, HA-HA!

J-JUST LIKE AKILAH MADE ME PRACTICE...

...

BU-BUMP

BU-BUMP

HHUH

HUH

BU-BUMP

HEY, FATSO, *SAY* SOMETHING.

JUST...JUST TELL THEM—

SNERK

ARE YOU FOR **REAL**?

...

CAN YOU **BELIEVE** THIS WIMP?

WEH-WEH-WEH, MY LIFE IS HELL. PWEEZE STAAAHP.

...

HA HA

REALAAAX!

WE'RE JUST HAVING FUN WITH YOU!

IT'S...

IT'S NOT FUN FOR **ME**!

WELL, THEN LIGHTEN UP!

YOINK

...!

H-HEY!

GIVE THEM BACK!

I NEED THEM!

D'URR, LOOK AT ME. I'M JENSEN!

WEH-WEH. I NEED THEM!

UH...

H-HEY, LET'S JUST GO, MAN.

GIVE THEM BACK.

WHAAAT? IT'S FUNNY!

JUST... JUST GIVE THEM BACK.

...

WHAT'S YOUR DEAL?

I JUST WANNA GO, OKAY?

GIVE HIM BACK HIS STUFF.

FINE. *SCOFF*

TOSS

FETCH, FOUR-EYES.

KTK

CLINK

NO!

DUDE, YOU BROKE THEM!!

....!

N-NO, I DIDN'T!

THEY MUST'VE BEEN ALREADY BROKEN!

ENOUGH.

YOU ERASE THAT VIDEO, OR I'LL—

HEY, WHAT'S ALL THIS YELLING?

WHAT'S GOING ON HERE?

u-uh.

...YANIC?

...

...

...

I THINK THIS CAN BE FIXED...

SPOILER ALERT— YANIC COULDN'T FIND A GOOD EXCUSE TO WEASEL OUT OF THIS ONE.

BOTH HE AND FOSTER GOT SUSPENDED.
I DON'T KNOW FOR HOW LONG.

NO ONE PETITIONED
TO BRING THEM BACK.

MR. R FIXED
MY GLASSES...

I DROP MINE ALL THE TIME, HEH.

JUST GOTTA POP THE LENS BACK IN.

...AND AFTER THE SCHOOL ADMIN SAW THE YANIC VIDEO AND JENNY AND AKILAH'S SOCIAL STUDY...

LIZARD BRAIN CULTURE: BULLYING AND ISOLATION

...THEY FREAKED OUT AND LAUNCHED A SCHOOL-WIDE "BULLYING AWARENESS AND PREVENTION" PROGRAM...

THIS IS DR. NUNEZ, A PSYCHOLOGIST. SHE'S HERE TO TALK TO YOU ABOUT—

...WITH, LIKE, CLASS SPEAKERS, "EMPATHY BUILDING" WORKSHOPS...

...AND REALLY WEIRD "TRUST-BUILDING" EXERCISES.

NOW PUT YOUR EGG ON THE SPOON AND GIVE IT TO YOUR PARTNER!

...

what.

hahaha

...I DUNNO IF IT'LL HELP...

...BUT I GUESS IT'S NICE OF THEM TO TRY.

...AND ONE GOOD THING DID COME OUT OF IT ALREADY.

H-HEY, JENSEN.

UH.

Y-YOU KNOW I DON'T **REALLY** MEAN ALL THAT STUFF I SAY TO YOU, RIGHT?

THAT I'M KIDDING?

...!

UH.

I GUESS?

...

I DON'T REALLY LIKE THOSE TYPES OF JOKES THOUGH.

C-COULD YOU STOP?

OH.

S-SURE.

WHATEVER.

229

SHE DIDN'T TALK TO ME FOR A WEEK AFTER THAT...

...WHICH WAS A BUMMER...

...BUT STILL BETTER THAN THE "JOKES."

...AND THEN, ON MONDAY—!

HEY, JENSEN, I THINK I MISSED YOUR BIRTHDAY THIS YEAR.

HOPE YOU LIKE CHOCOLATE!

...TL;DR— WE GET ALONG MUCH BETTER NOW...

...AND THE DAILY SCHOOL LEVEL GOT EASIER.

HI, JENSEN!

H-HEY.

...

HEY.

OH, HI, OLIVIA! HI, GUYS.

? ? ?

THE GAME MONSTERS ARE VERY CONFUSED.

...I WONDER NOW... IF THEY WERE EVEN MONSTERS AT ALL...

...OR JUST REGULAR PLAYERS, SAME AS EVERYONE ELSE...

DOES SHE EXPECT **ALL** THIS BY **TOMORROW**?

NO WAY...

...SIMPLY TRYING TO GET THROUGH MIDDLE SCHOOL.

....!

...FOSTER'S BACK?

...HE SEEMS DIFFERENT.

HEY, WEASEL, YOU'RE BACK.

WHERE'S YOUR BUDDY— HE LEFT YOU ALL ALONE?

U-UH... HE'S STILL SUSPENDED, I THINK.

HA-HA, SERVES THAT RODENT RIGHT!

SEE YOU AT LUNCH, WASTE OF SPACE!

SHOVE

....!

. . .

SLAM

...I USED TO KINDA THINK THAT EVERYONE KNEW HOW TO GET THROUGH MIDDLE SCHOOL EXCEPT FOR ME...

...THAT THEY ALL HAD CHEAT CODES OR SOMETHING...

...AND KNEW SOME SECRET MOVES I DIDN'T.

JENSEN.

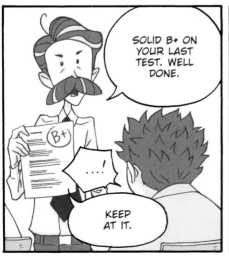

SOLID B+ ON YOUR LAST TEST. WELL DONE.

....!

KEEP AT IT.

...NOW I THINK WE'RE ALL JUST TRYING TO FIGURE THIS OUT...

...LEVELING UP, ONE LITTLE VICTORY AT A TIME...

...AND HOW IT'S ALWAYS BEEN AROUND, IN SOME FORM...

GROUP PRESENTATIONS TODAY

MAJOR LEAGUE BASEBALL USED TO NOT LET YOU PLAY UNLESS YOU WERE WHITE AND MALE, UNTIL—

...AND HOW IT DOES GET CHANGED OVER TIME, JUST LIKE AKILAH SAID.

BUD FOWLER

ELIZABETH "LIZZIE" MURPHY

TONI STONE

PEOPLE CHANGING IT, WITH THEIR ACTIONS—

IN 19 FOWL BECA

...

I WONDER IF THEY WERE EVER SCARED, TRYING TO CHANGE THINGS.

RRINNG

CHATTER

HA HA HA

BERRYBROOK SCHOOL

hey

235

...I DIDN'T END UP LIKING "MY BADLY DRAWN LIFE" AT ALL...

...BUT I LOVE INA CRUZ'S BOOKS.

"FIGHTER" IS MY FAVORITE ONE.

SHE TALKS A LOT ABOUT ALL THAT STUFF IN IT—

—ABOUT FIXING WHAT'S WRONG, CHANGING WHAT'S AROUND YOU, DOING THINGS YOU'RE AFRAID OF...

...ABOUT WHAT COURAGE IS.

"IT'S EASY TO GROW BITTER, TO RETREAT INTO YOURSELF, AFTER BEING REJECTED.

"IT'S SCARY TO KEEP REACHING OUT, TO KEEP EXTENDING YOUR HAND, AFTER SO MANY WOULD NOT TAKE IT...AND SOMETIMES EVEN PUSH IT AWAY...

"...BUT THAT'S WHAT COURAGE IS—NOT NEVER BEING AFRAID...

SURVEY QUESTION:
What culture would **YOU** want to build? What would be the norm there?

Which actions would help build this culture?

"...BUT BEING AFRAID AND DOING IT ANYWAY..."

"...TO KEEP REACHING OUT TO THE WORLD THAT WOULD NOT HAVE YOU...

INHALE

"...AND SAYING, 'LET'S BE FRIENDS.'

"BECAUSE WE ARE ALL STRONGER—

"—WHEN WE ALL LOOK OUT FOR ONE ANOTHER.

THE END

...ALSO, THE **SUNSPOTS!** THE SUNSPOTS ARE VERY IMPORTANT. PLEASE KEEP AN EYE OUT FOR THOSE!!

JUST TEN MORE YEARS UNTIL I CAN APPLY TO NASA, AND THEN I'LL TAKE CARE OF THEM. JUST GOTTA LEARN MORE MATH FIRST.

JENSEN GRAHAM, REGULAR MIDDLE SCHOOLER AND FUTURE NASA ASTRONAUT— OVER AND OUT.

NOW, THE END. (FOR REAL.)

CONGRATULATIONS!!!

(to me, for finishing making this book, and to you, for finishing reading it! ☺)

At this point you're probably <u>seriously</u> wondering 'what's the deal with these sunspots?!' Why does Jensen care about them so much?!' Well, the back story here is that Jensen was doing research for a science class project once upon a time, about our solar system and especially the sun. To his SHOCK and HORROR, Jensen discovered the existence of...

SUNSPOTS!!!

(areas of high magnetic activity on the surface of the sun that precede)

CORONAL MASS EJECTION!! 😨

(basically giant flaming tentacles of SUN STUFF that shoot out into space)

Jensen's fear is that one of these solar events could one day reach the Earth... And FRY IT TO A CRISP.

SIZZLE

EARTH

NO NO NO NOoo

...so this is why he wants to work for NASA, to find a fix for that.

(IMPORTANT NOTE:
To my knowledge all that stuff is not a real danger to Earth, so hopefully Jensen is in for a pleasant surprise!)

Having said that, I can definitely relate to dealing with a deep-seated fear. (who doesn't have one?! They're lucky!) When I was about 11-12 years old, I was terrified of a large open maintenance well on the edge of my town.

It was an 8-10 foot drop to a strong foaming roar of dark rushing water.

I was so afraid, I could barely breathe whenever I passed it — what if the water started rising? We lived near a dam and the water from the lake could totally flood my entire little town. I'd lie awake at night, wondering if it was going to happen NOW, while everyone slept. Was the dark cold water rising out of the well?!

(Spoiler—it wasn't. But I still had to slink out of my comfy bed to check and make sure.)

As I got older and learned more about the water systems in my town, I realized that what I was so afraid of couldn't really happen, phew! It's weird how learning about the thing you're afraid of can actually help you get over the fear.

... Well, that, and copious amounts of daydreaming and drawing. Which, like Jensen, I did a lot of, on a daily basis (and also mostly in school, hahaaaaaa ...)

... AND NOW I'M AN INTERNATIONALLY PUBLISHED AUTHOR OF 12+ BOOKS so that all worked out okay. 😄👍

Moral of this long-winded story: if you're afraid of sunspots and stupid creepy maintenance wells on edges of small towns, you may have a bright future as a writer and/or cartoonist?! Stranger things have happened.

AND NOW!!! It's time for the...

SKETCH GALLERY!!

Before I start drawing a book, I always do tons of what is called 'concept sketching'.

It's basically a lot of loose, fast doodling, where the artist will try out some visuals of character ideas. And by loose doodling I mean loose. Barely legible. Downright horrible, really; so bad that I won't even include them here because I don't want you to go blind. YOU ARE WELCOME.

... But here are some rough sketches that are a step up from that and safe to look at:

Mrs. Crabbler was a lot of fun to design. She didn't end up in a lot of scenes in the book, so I was trying to capture her whole character/role in just a couple of self-explanatory drawings.

Jensen!!

I loved drawing Jensen SO. MUCH. I wish I could do a whole book of just his amazing daydream adventures in space, where he fights Mars zombies and discovers extraterrestrial civilizations.

Mrs. Crabbler's sister?!

no idea

Not all teacher designs made it into the book, but I still had fun sketching them. Better too many designs than not enough!!

Expressions are 99.999% of what makes a character, IMHO.

So I draw A LOT of them.

Jenny and Akilah, the BFF series

reading comics, listening to music together

Felipe ← colour streaks in hair?

Very early newspaper crew sketches, just trying to get their personalities down, very loosely.

...And, last but not least, no sketch gallery is complete without Mr. Raccoon!

☆ THANK YOU! ☆

... to my husband, Patrick, who would bring me food and make sure I had everything I needed during the last relentless deadline dash; to Melissa, who REALLY burned that midnight oil to help color this book on top of everything else she had going on; to my editor, JuYoun, for too many things to count but especially for getting me more time; to my publisher, Kurt, for the faith in the face of no discernable pages ಠ‿ಠ; to the AMAZING Yen Press crew for making my stuff look professional and awesome; to Nancy, for the inside info on the nurse's office particulars; to my agent, Judy, for always looking out for me; and last but not least...

THANK YOU to all my family, friends, and fans who make the lonely hard work of making a graphic novel bearable and totally worth it.

♡ ♡ ♡ Luv,
Svetlana

March 9th, 2017

It all started with **awkward** and continues with **crush**!

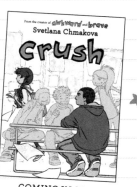

AVAILABLE NOW!

COMING IN 2018!